STORIES MY FATHER TOLD ME

"Experience the American dream. *Stories My Father Told Me* chronicles a family's epic journey from Eastern European shtetls to mid-twentieth century New York. Haskell Brodsky's entrepreneurial spirit fuels this heartwarming saga of immigration, resilience, and the pursuit of a better future. Filled with vivid characters and historical detail, this novel captures the struggles and triumphs of building a new life in America."

—**BARBARA BOWMAN**, TV PRODUCER, ENTREPRENEUR

"A timeless tale of family and resilience perfect for fans of historical fiction. This novel will inspire, entertain, and resonate deeply."

—**CAROLYN CLARKE**, BEST-SELLING AUTHOR OF *AND THEN THERE'S MARGARET*

"From shtetl to skyscrapers. Follow Haskell Brodsky's unexpected rise from a poor young tailor in Poland to head of a thriving entrepreneurial empire in Manhattan. *Stories My Father Told Me* weaves together tales of love, loss, and community, with colorful characters, the resilience of a family navigating the complexities of tradition and progress, and even a dose of the mob! A captivating story of courage, wit, and the enduring grit of the human spirit."

—**AMY POWERS**, BEST-SELLING AUTHOR OF *NO DEGREE REQUIRED*, HEALTH AND WELLNESS MULTIPRENEUR

"Seymour Ubell's tender storytelling celebrates the bonds of love that bind us together and the resilience of the human spirit in the face of sorrow. This page-turner will stay with you long after the final page."

—**MICHAEL BEAS**, CEO AND FOUNDER OF *THE BOOK REVUE*

STORIES
MY FATHER
TOLD
ME

a novel

SEYMOUR UBELL

Stories My Father Told Me
© 2025 Seymour Ubell

Hardcover ISBN: 979-8-9925409-0-1
Paperback ISBN: 979-8-9925409-1-8
Ebook ISBN: 979-8-9925409-2-5

Cover design by Claudine Mansour Designs

Published by Madison & Mulholland Publishing

MADISON &
MULHOLLAND

I dedicate this book to my wife, Marsha; my children, Lynn, Jane, and Edward, and their spouses, Rick and Erin; my grandchildren, Matt and Laurie, Javier and Karoline, Ben, Alex, and Ellie, and my great-granddaughter, Ida; also, my brothers, Earl, Alvin, and Robert, and my sister-in-law, Rosalyn. A special thank you to my daughter Jane, an amazing woman whose guidance and literary skills were a mountain of help.

PROLOGUE

I am Eric Brodsky, Haskell's eldest son. This is our story, the yearning and hardships my family endured and its history. A tale of the Yuboroffsky clan, a Polish/Romanian Jewish family's European history, and its progression into America's mid-twentieth century. They created extraordinary lives, filled with love, kindness, success, and as in all life-spans and households, their own spells of pain and tragedy.

This is my version of our story, a chronicle and a reconstruction of tales passed through five generations, from my great-great-grandfather Havrohm, to my great-grandfather Moishe, to my grandfather Solomon, then to me from my own father, Haskell. It is an unforgettable American account, the miracle of peasants and their determination to succeed while treasuring the family they created.

My father and other Jewish immigrants settled in New York City in the early 1920s a few streets away from tenements on such fabled streets as Delancey, Essex, and Rivington. Italian families settled nearby, and I came to understand their histories in the same light as ours. Working class families, the poor. All racing from persecution in the Old Country with hope in their hearts and encountering similar challenges in America. They, too, our co-passengers, carried a sea of dreams and an ocean of hope. Italian, Polish, Scandinavian: all experienced similar fears in their struggle to survive. Threats from rival gangs and organized crime swept the city.

When I was a teen, my friend Naldo Pucci had a story similar to ours. His was the only Italian family in our otherwise Jewish neighborhood. They were originally brought to America by his grandfather Salvatore to New York's Little Italy on Mulberry Street, where they still faced discrimination, this time from the police, gangsters, and tough factory bosses. Threads of our stories intertwine, as we shall see. Our experiences blend and merge into many immigrants' similar efforts to make the American dream come true.

CHAPTER 1

SEPTEMBER 1923, FROM POLAND TO ELLIS ISLAND

My father, Haskell, stood against the ship's railing to breathe in fresh, chilly air, a relief from the dense stink in steerage. He watched Europe's coast fade into the distance, and his past in Suwalki, Poland, gone.

In their midsized town, the synagogue was near the family's modest tailoring shop. Each of the shops had common craftsmen with uncommon skills in hand-sewing and worked equally as well on the new-fangled machines. Like many, they toiled to escape their peasant roots and the strangulation of poverty. Their demanding work included their wives, daughters, and sons as they struggled to make ends meet.

Still, they were not sheltered from the ravages of hatred. Hanging over any shred of normalcy was the constant threat of pogroms, the organized massacres of Jews in Russia and Eastern Europe. The lifelong fear and the danger of the attacks did not abate for years and grew more threatening with each generation.

Haskell left behind the history of four Yuboroffsky generations. His family's dedicated work ethic had built a successful tailoring business in their shtetl, and they hoped to bring Haskell's father, Solomon, into the business that his grandfather Havrohm Yuboroffsky, and his father, Moishe, had labored to build on only a needle, a thread, and a button.

Despite his best intentions, Solomon was not destined to become a great tailor.

Moishe smiled and said, "A mensch tracht un Gott lacht [a man plans, and God laughs]."

Turning to his father, Solomon whispered with respect and admiration, "You are a tailor—the best tailor in our village. What will I be when I am your age?"

"You, my son, are a blessed young man, thank God," Moishe said. "You are filled with smiles and happy words. From your lips a funny story tumbles and people laugh. Everyone has loved you since you were a child. And now, you are a man, and you should continue with those gifts. A tailor you will never be . . . but a businessman you shall become!"

Haskell leaned into the damp winds of the Baltic Sea, knowing he might never hear his father telling his favorite stories again, knowing that the voice to tell those stories would now be his own.

THE SOLOMON STORY

Solomon set out to train himself. He walked the streets of Suwalki, calling out, shouting to the townsfolk in a strong, earnest voice, "The best women's dresses and men's coats! Warm winter jackets! Beautiful dresses with fine tailoring at the lowest prices!" With his smooth, flowing voice and constant smile, Solomon brought a new sound and sight to the streets of Suwalki, drawing people to their windows, passersby waving approval, and women interrupting their chores to look.

After his first disappointing week, failure hung on his face. Adding to an aching back, he did not have a single sale. The second week, pedestrians gawked. "Who is this mashuga boychik [insane boy]?" His street routine threatened to become tragic and pitiful.

At the end of each day, Solomon was both confused and exhausted. However, he refused to be defeated. His inner voice guided him to a different approach, and he hired a boy to carry a huge sign across his shoulders that read: "Fine Tailoring! Best Clothes! Excellent Prices!" Laughter and finger-pointing trailed the boy; nothing came of it. Repeatedly stymied, Solomon earned only sleepless nights and crushing doubts.

Moishe believed in his son, but it did not keep him from scolding the boy: "There is no surrender," he shouted. "You cannot and will not give up. You must have faith in yourself, and only then you will succeed," he thundered. "The word 'no' cannot live in your heart or young mind, not for a single moment."

Solomon kept calling out, street after street, and became distracted by the attractive young women passing by. He forgot his disappointment and fell into silence, staring at one young woman in particular. He gave her a grin, and the beauty responded with a slight smile. A welcome yearning filled him and a strange gut feeling inspired him to hire this angel-faced girl of sixteen, whom he dressed in fine garments—a tailored coat over a tweed jacket and skirt. She brushed her hair, put on a touch of lip rouge, and the experiment began.

The young beauty paraded around with Solomon and captivated the quaint city. He could not have predicted the response from the townspeople. All took notice! They oohed and aahed as they gazed at the lovely young woman dressed so elegantly. One by one they came closer to admire her. Many rubbed the fine fabrics between their thumb and forefinger. They tugged at the seams and evaluated the buttons, and Solomon felt his first stroke of success. Still, he was cautious and protected his companion as well as his garments from any unwelcome attention.

Zosia, another striking young woman from a different village, enchanted the townspeople as she strutted with confidence, beauty, and elegance, attracting customers. Her effect was a revelation for the fledging seller. This new strategy, a marvel, a magical moment of how to succeed, had almost eluded him. The attention-grabbing gambit became the pivotal power of the future, attracting new customers. Zosia was the magnet and cornerstone in the growth of the family tailor shop.

On the heels of success, Solomon hired two additional striking young women. Anastaza and Maja were outfitted in dresses, suits, and coats. A young man, Filip, handsome with a look of elegance, joined them in a fine suit as they paraded throughout Suwalki. They became the shop's first models (a word that did not exist in those days) and were followed and approached by the curious—all potential customers—to whom Solomon presented his handmade business card.

Soon the little tailor shop in the village filled with customers laughing, gossiping, and placing orders. The shop was enlarged by renting another store next door, which doubled the space. Now our historic Yuboroffsky Tailor Shop, in all honesty, could be called a business. A first step into an unknown future.

There was no way to know what would happen to his family or the Yuboroffsky Tailor Shop that Haskell left behind in Suwalki. A sadness opened deep in him as the distance from his family widened. He was committed to his goal to break out and escape the persecution plaguing his town and much of Poland. It took all the strength and courage he could muster to leave his homeland for places unknown, as his older brothers Abe and Label had done two years before him.

CHAPTER 2

OFF TO AMERICA

The ship to America was crowded with strangers from every oppressed, depressed, and desolate part of Europe. Many families from the Old Country, like Haskell's, could only afford to travel in steerage, where food and provisions and comforts were scarce.

Mothers, teary-eyed, clutched infants tightly, pressing them against their breasts. Youngsters of all ages boarded the giant ship step by step. Heads down, two and three abreast were starting a mysterious, life-changing adventure. Pale-faced teenagers clung to Momma and Poppa, their hands gripping the freezing side rails. One fearful moment after another they all lurched upward along the narrow gangplank. Elderly relatives with canes in hand followed haltingly. Who could predict that this courageous decision would save their lives and those who followed? All were fortunate: the risk of living in America was worth the gamble. They conquered the dread and the pain of leaving their families behind and did not dream that their fearlessness would change the destiny of their heirs. Their courageous risk-taking gave them the opportunity to take their lives to America and reap the possible rewards of a better life in the New World.

The ship's officer called out, his lips on his bullhorn, "All aboard!"

Many faces were etched with determination, steeling themselves for the steerage bunks and oppressive seasickness that lay ahead. They moved, step by step, determined and tormented by memories of their past perils and those they may face in the unknown land. This voyage carried frightening dangers. Each person gathered their strength and their hopes as they heroically faced the consequences of their irreversible choice. The mystery of their future now outweighed the history of their past, a time when they faced each day with the agony and desperation that propelled them to this point. Among the many lures to America was the promise of freedom and the possibility of prosperity.

• • •

In this cramped setting, there were hardships and hopes, contrasts and conflicts. Haskell, my father, was a reserved twenty-year-old, slight of build, who kept to himself until he couldn't. On the fourth day, from his bunk, he heard a young woman cry out: "Take your filthy hands off me. You disgust me!" A large man groped her again. She broke free and fled past my father's bunk.

Haskell stepped out into the path of her pursuer. "Tell me, sir, would this be your wife or your daughter?" he said politely.

The towering Goliath bellowed, "Stand aside, you little shit! This is none of your damned business!"

"Ah, but it is my business!" he said, placing a friendly touch on the young woman's shoulder. "I know she's not related to you because this girl is my friend's sister. I promised him I would watch over her during our voyage." A lie, but a noble one.

The room silenced; all eyes focused on the danger befalling the misjudgment of this audacious young man. During the voyage, this Cossack monster had been marked by his aggressive behavior, leering and touching women and threatening any man in his way. The bully, face-to-face and within an inch of Haskell's nose, roared, "Mind your own fuckin' business, or I'll beat your moron brains out."

As David to Goliath, Haskell stood fearlessly, holding his breath and hiding a slight tremble. He said simply, "You will have to do more than that." His voice came from deep within him, both steady and firm.

"What is your puny, empty mind thinking, boy?" the hulk asked.

Haskell did not waver. "What I am thinking," he said, then paused, "is that beating my moronic brains out is not enough to end your problems. You will have to kill me. Because if you don't, I will kill you."

The Giant was amused and snorted, "And how will you do that? I can crush you with one hand." He chuckled in a tone that sounded like a storm.

With the chutzpah [nerve] of David, Haskell faced his Goliath. "When you are asleep," he said in a soft, unfrightened tone, "I will silently slip by your bed, a sharp knife in my hand, and while everyone sleeps, I will plunge my knife into your throat. And all your good friends, here in this cabin, each one of them, will happily help me push your cut-up body through the portholes of this ship to feed the fish."

A collective gasp spread through the cabin, all eyes watching the two. The young woman, one hand to her mouth, the other hand clutching Haskell, quivered as she shut her eyes to an invisible darkness.

An unexpected smile cracked the lips of the monster's face. It was a first for him. *This skinny kid has guts and nerve.* He scowled, and with a mock cuff to his young adversary's shoulder, started to laugh. "Let's have a drink! I like your courage." He turned away. "I have good Russian vodka in my suitcase!"

And so, the tense moment passed. The hazards of Cossack treachery from the Old Country that hung over the passengers dissolved. Haskell was celebrated for his courage, which added a little swagger to his step.

As the ship came within reach of America, optimism swelled in the hearts of everyone on board. The first glimpse of their future was stamped with tears, cheering, jumping, waving, and laughing as the colossus of the Statue of Liberty came into sight. The ship sailed into Ellis Island, and here the impoverished, the struggling, the downtrodden were pronounced reborn into a new life with the indelible proclamation engraved on the statue's base from a poem by the Jewish poet Emma Lazarus:

> Give me your tired, your poor,
> Your huddled masses yearning to breathe free,
> The wretched refuse of your teeming shore.
> Send these, the homeless, tempest-tost to me,
> I lift my lamp beside the golden door!

Haskell Yuboroffsky, one more excited passenger among the many, felt the elation of sailing inches from the Statue of Liberty and into New York Harbor. His fellow travelers, fists against their breasts, hungered for just one tiny touch of her beautiful hand, which was held high, welcoming all.

Like many at the Ellis Island émigré entry port, the inspector looked at Haskell's birth name on his passport and determined his name would be unpronounceable in America. He suspected but did not know that this youth, full of vim and vigor, did not understand a word of English.

Searching his face, the Ellis Island wizard posed the question, "Are you planning to live in America, learn English, and be a good citizen?" In response, Haskell instinctively smiled and nodded his approval.

The inspector waved his magical hand, stamped Haskell's documents and wrote in English, "Haskell Brodsky." The uniformed virtuoso said, "You are now in America with an American name. Welcome." He looked past Haskell and waved to the next potential American. "Next!"

CHAPTER 3

ADJUSTING TO AMERICA

The newly named Haskell Avram Brodsky commingled tears with his brother Abraham, who came to greet him. The brothers' reunion on the other side of the Atlantic, on American soil, was a historic moment in their lives, a turning point at the start of their new future together. Abe had arrived two years earlier and lived as most immigrant Jewish families did then, in a tiny apartment on Manhattan's Lower East Side with Ida, his new wife.

"I am happy you are here at last, my brother, unharmed," Abe said. "You must be tired and should rest. In a few days, we will help you find work and friends to help you adjust to your new home."

"Abe! I have a new name!" Haskell grinned. He knew his new name would provoke a reaction, so he turned his papers over to his older brother.

Abe shook the papers angrily. "What is this Haskell Brodsky? That is not your name! We are Yuboroffsky, are we not?"

Haskell smirked. "They gave me an *American* name!"

Abe paused, considering the judgment of the Ellis Island official. Then he handed the name-changing immigration document to Ida, who shrugged. "Good idea," she said.

Ida blinked and smiled. "Abe, let's change our name also to Brodsky! It sounds more American!"

"Yes. Let's do it! Our new name for our new nation!"

And so, it was. Our ancestral name disappeared, and we were now and forever, Brodsky.

CHAPTER 4

THEIR NEW YORK LIFE

In New York, Abe and my father, Haskell, were now out of harm's way—or so it seemed. The pogroms were behind them, but this land had its own dangers. Criminal Jewish gangs, factory bosses, and street hoodlums all waited to prey on the gullible new arrivals.

Already a skilled sewing machine operator, it took Haskell a few weeks to secure a position at a lady's dress factory. He was one of three men and thirty women who worked on sewing machines. They were called pieceworkers, and their earnings depended on how many dresses they completed each day. The sewing floor brimmed with hundreds of garments hanging on racks and bustled with the shuttling of items from one work area to the next, from cutting to sewing and then from trimming, to cleaning, to pressing, and finally to brushing and touching up details like buttons, hems, and shoulders.

On the cutting floor above were all the men; their gestures with long, sharp scissors seemed to move in tandem. They fell upon layers of cloth, often ten to fifteen layers high. They cut the cloth according to the pattern paper on top of the fabric with chalk marks and efficiently moved the cut stacks of cloth to the side to be gathered and delivered downstairs to the sewing machine operators.

Overseeing the sewing floor was Mr. Lefkowitz, a bearded, scull-capped, scowling supervisor. His forays and bullying up and down the aisles brought unwelcome intrusions on the young women busily attending to their sewing machines. He frequently moved his fingers across the women's backs and often onto their bosoms. He leaned over their shoulders, his smelly, hot breath on their cheeks. These frightened ladies held back their embarrassment and anger, pretending nothing was happening rather than risk losing their jobs.

His all too frequent fondling of the young women eventually met with an outburst of resistance. Teresa, for whom the supervisor had taken a special liking, erupted when once too often she felt his unwelcome touch on her breast. In a burst of anger, she shoved back her stool, stood, and screamed, "Take your filthy hands off me. You are a disgusting animal!"

The women around her gasped. Teresa shouted, "You can feel or touch any of the women in this shop, but you'd better leave me alone. My boyfriend told me if you do it again, he will come here and beat your brains in. And if you dare fire me, he said he will kill you," she raged, expanding her invention of her strong and protective boyfriend.

The humming of all the machines in the room fell silent. Mr. Lefkowitz, shocked at this outburst and red-faced, retreated to his office, slamming the door behind him. It was unheard of; no one ever dared to speak to him that way. The tension was broken by quiet applause and nervous laughter from the ladies in the shop. The three sewing machine men all smiled.

The threat of Teresa's invented boyfriend worked. She emerged with her honor and her job and earned the admiration of her fellow workers. Afterward, to the great relief of the other women, the supervisor ceased "accidentally" touching anyone.

Two Italian boys, no more than fifteen years old, fanned out over the two factory floors cleaning and picking up pieces of cloth and other rubbish. It made no difference how hard they worked; the shop was always filthy. The poor labor conditions meant grimy windows and stinking latrines. The rooms were either stifling with the summer heat or freezing in winter. The patterns the garment industry cut became the blueprint of their exploitation. Bosses had an endless surplus of workers in the limitless onrush of poor immigrants desperate to find footing away from the pogroms and anti-Semitism across autocratic Europe and Russia. Jobs were scarce—workers, many.

Haskell made friends quickly among the garment workers. The traits he inherited from his grandfather Moishe and father, Solomon, served him well. His humor and diligence brought him to the attention of Mr. Ginsberg, the big boss and owner, who one day called him into his office. They spoke in Yiddish.

"Haskell, you are a good worker, and you leave people with a happy feeling after their lunch as they come back to work. I've seen it. I like it. And I like you. I am going to give you a two-dollar a week raise." The owner spoke kindly and with a sense of respect. "For your future, I suggest that you go to school at night to improve your English." Mr. Ginsberg paused. "And one more thing, this is serious. Do not tell anyone about the extra money I am giving you."

Haskell was puzzled by the pledge to tell no one. He returned in a slight daze to his sewing station. He resumed working, his face pale and unsmiling. The young woman working at the machine beside him took notice.

"Haskell, are you all right?"

He nodded.

"You don't look all right. Did the boss fire you or give you a cut?"

"Shh, shh." He turned his head, looking around. "The boss just told me to learn English."

"He must like you a lot! It's a good sign and a wonderful idea. I'm doing it myself after work. If you want to, you can come with me. I go three nights a week to the public school only two blocks away."

On the subway home, Haskell convinced himself that his promise to Mr. Ginsberg meant not to tell anyone at work. That evening, upon returning home, he confided in Abe, relating what happened. Abe listened carefully and said he agreed with Mr. Ginsberg, encouraging his brother to study English.

Abe considered the young woman and her invitation. "Tell me, the girl that you will be going to school with, is she Jewish?"

Haskell grinned and nodded, the color rising in his cheeks.

"What is her name?"

"Her name is Molly. And by the way, I don't need the extra two dollars. I'll bring the extra money to Ida for some of the expenses."

Abe brightened. "Good idea. Ida will be happy!"

CHAPTER 5

Molly and Haskell worked their way through the language lessons, which they regarded as the gateway to the American dream. They traded their new vocabulary words with one another as they tried on colloquial phrases and teased each other in English. Digesting the new language knitted them closer and closer, and as their fluency grew, so did their relationship.

After several months, Molly let Haskell hold her hand, and a few weeks later, he kissed the woman who would eventually become his wife.

One morning Haskell strode with assurance into Mr. Ginsberg's office and greeted him with perfect enunciation. "Good morning, Mr. Ginsberg. I take it you are having a good day?"

The boss laughed good-naturedly at the contrast between the young man's attempts at formal English and his Polish accent. Mr. Ginsberg motioned Haskell to take a seat. "Your English is good. I am pleased. I know you are smart and a quick learner, so I have decided to put you into my cutting room, which is a big promotion. But I want you to know, you will have to join the union."

Haskell struggled to stay calm. *The union*, he thought. *Oy vey! This will mean a big raise. Maybe I can ask Molly to marry me.* His brain flooded with dreams. He thanked Mr. Ginsberg and nearly tripped over the threshold as he hurried to Molly.

"I can't wait until lunch to tell you."

"What is it?" she asked, her eyes widening.

"Mr. Ginsberg wants me to be a cutter and join the union."

"That's wonderful! I am so proud of you!" Molly held her breath.

Haskell could hardly speak. "Here is what is more wonderful: I will get an eleven-dollar a week raise. It's a small fortune."

Molly put her hand to her breast to hold herself upright as her thoughts spun around themselves. She took a step toward him and interlaced her fingers behind his neck. "I love you," she whispered.

"I love you back. Let's get married!" The proposal flew from his mouth, zipping past his lips.

Molly beamed. "Let me speak to my parents. They might think it's too soon or I'm too young."

"Let me join you. I want to meet your momma and poppa, and it's important that they know I have the courage to ask them face-to-face. And that I will make enough to support both of us. Together we will manage."

They shared an excited kiss then looked around to see two of the nearby operators smile. Hand in hand, they headed back to work. Molly proceeded to the sewing shop and Haskell went to the cutting floor, invigorated by the possibilities and the life that lay before them.

CHAPTER 6

Months passed. Molly stood outside Ginsberg's office door. Taking a deep breath. Her heart beating loud enough for all to hear. With eyes shut tight, she knocked on the open door. Mr. Ginsberg looked up. "Ah, yes. Molly. Come in."

She stood before him with all the courage she could muster, trembling.

"Molly, what's on your mind? Are you quitting?" he joked.

"No, Mr. Ginsberg, I am not leaving you. May I please have a few minutes?" She spoke in almost perfect English with a slight Polish accent.

"Ah, your English is quite good. Where did you learn?" he asked.

"Haskell and I go to the same school three nights a week," she said, immediately regretting it.

Ginsberg smiled, totally understanding. It happened often in his factory; boy meets girl. He remembered seeing his Rachel and falling in love in this very factory that his father began. He gave Molly a knowing smile. "What's on your mind, Molly?"

She began her well-planned, well-rehearsed story of her life. "I was born in Warsaw, the largest city in Poland. My grandfather, and then my father, ran the dry goods shop they owned for more than forty-six years. I worked there often. I did sales, alterations of clothing, sweeping, and most importantly, I took care of the books and all the money."

She hesitated. "I am smart. I work hard. I am ready to end my piecework in your shop. And now my question. Is there a place in your office for me so I can change my job in the factory and do for you what I did for my poppa's business?"

Ginsberg was not surprised. He was pleased that this young immigrant girl had the determination to do better for herself. He recalled his own fear when asking his father for a change in his job from the cutting room to another part of the business. It was like yesterday that he shuddered as he spoke to his father on the subway. It was a horror. And like his dad, the surprise was that his father smiled at his son's tenacity. Molly stood before him with the same look of resolve.

Ginsberg remained silent. His thoughts swerved in multiple directions. His quality control manager, Harry, needed additional coaching and training. The girl standing before him would be able to relax his bookkeeping chores, and he would be able to spend the free time giving Harry the guidance that his father had given him. In his mind, it was done.

He was impressed with Molly and her guts. He also knew her work ethic; she was a major producer in the shop. She had presented this solution herself, and it was perfect timing.

"And so, Molly," he began, "it happens that I do have a place for you in my office if you are capable. But first let's talk about money. How much do you earn with your piecework?" Mr. Ginsberg knew what was going to happen, and he was prepared to make Molly an offer. Molly knew exactly how much she earned last week and the week before. "Last week, I earned eighteen dollars. And the week before, seventeen dollars and sixty-five cents."

He sat quietly thinking, then responded, "Starting on Monday, you will begin at twenty dollars each week." He smiled.

"Mr. Ginsberg, the job is worth twenty-three dollars a week."

And suddenly his smile disappeared. He was shocked to hear her answer. He remained silent. *Ah, what a wonderful girl. Perfect,* he thought. "Twenty-one and not a penny more."

"Twenty-two," she countered. "I know how to manage the books and keep watch on the inventory. You can do no better than to hire me."

Ginsberg did not answer. His heart smiled. He put his hand out to Molly and beamed. "OK, OK, you got it. Start Monday at eight."

She jumped from her chair in a burst of excitement and gave him a surprise hug. Molly gathered herself as she left his office with no smile, no expression. She did not want any coworkers to ask any questions.

Ginsberg chuckled. *Haskell's girlfriend was indeed a treasure.*

CHAPTER 7

MY STORY AS A BOY

Poppa Haskell poked my shoulder as I slept. I shared a room with my younger brother, Ely, where our mother's sewing machine doubled as a table between our beds. My older sister, Hannahla, had a small room to herself.

She can have her own room, I thought, *because today, I, the favorite (in my mind alone), get to collaborate with my father. This is a treat, an honor. I am so happy to be invited by my father into a world I dreamed about with our grandfathers. The same thing happened to me that occurred with the same historic path taken by my grandfather Solomon, my great-grandfather Moishe, and started by my great-great-grandfather Havrohm.*

This Saturday morning, February 1945, was still dark. "Get up! Get up!" My father shook me. The original nudge didn't work. "It's time to go to work. I told you to go to bed early last night. But you wouldn't listen."

I groaned. Turned over. Hid my head under warm blankets.

"I'm going without you." Not in a whisper, yet not as a shout. He turned and left, going to our one bathroom. For a moment, my heroic hope disappeared. My sleep fought me. *Stay in bed*, my brain whispered. Going to work with my father was the winner. I blasted myself out of bed and grabbed my shirt and trousers.

Poppa had showered and was finished shaving when I went into the small toilet. I brushed my teeth, gazed into the mirror at my smooth face, and rubbed my chin with the open palm of my hand. *No stubble yet*, I thought sadly. I looked forward to lathering my face and shaving, just like my father. Instead, I washed, rinsed my mouth, and toweled off quickly. In fifteen minutes, I was ready to leave with Poppa, who strolled out of his room clean, handsome, and dressed like a banker.

I had agreed that each Saturday morning I would go to our factory in Manhattan, helping with customers who came to buy suits and coats at off-retail prices. Many bought a jacket with a pair of pants at wholesale prices, plus 15 percent, which was still a huge saving.

I could feel the outside chill on my forehead pressed against the windowpane. My gray flannel trousers and warm woolen winter jacket would be enough to ward off the cold on the ride to Poppa's factory. I secretly enjoyed my parents bragging about my dream to work in the family business. I dreamed of working with my dad and fell in love with helping in the shop. By the time I was a seventeen-year-old son who loved and admired his father, I alone was on the road to being Poppa's true partner.

We took a trolly car to Nostrand Avenue in Brooklyn and boarded the IRT subway to the factory at Union Square. Less trains ran on Saturdays, but they were still crowded enough that riders clung to the hanging leather straps. Poppa looked at me with a slight dip of his chin and nudged me. This quiet signal meant to get up and give my seat to the elderly gentleman standing in the middle of the subway car. And so, I did what was expected. He nodded and I did the same.

Every Saturday I would read the passing signs of each subway station as we sped by. It was a short walk to our factory at 100

Fifth Avenue near Fifteenth Street. We walked up the stairs of the subway and a blast of chilly wind hit our faces. "Poppa," I pleaded, "let's take a taxi—it's freezing out. It's eighteen degrees!" I trembled.

With an expression of both strength and smiles, he baited me: "You call this cold? You call this cold?" He repeated, "In Poland, we went swimming on a day like this!" He knew a good joke could help make all things more bearable, even shivering. Somewhere between intuition and implication, I felt that this familiar manner, which he used with his friends and employees, was meant to bond us, a signal that one day I would join in his business.

The elevator door opened to the sixth floor. With pride and purpose, Poppa took his place under the huge sign that read "Abraham & Haskell Corp., Men's Clothing." He unlocked the door and there we were.

"Good morning, Uncle Haskell. Good morning," Cousin Melvin, my Uncle Abe's son, called out. We half-heartedly returned his greeting.

Melvin had graduated from Brooklyn's Erasmus Hall High School. Now he was working in the shop full-time. I was jealous, although I shouldn't have been. Melvin had a heart murmur; it limited his ability to play sports and kept him out of the war.

Uncle Abe worked efficiently and obsessively to oversee everything. He took care of production, design, delivery, and, most importantly, paying the vendors and getting paid by the customers. On the other hand, he was quick to lose his temper, and his thunderous outbursts accompanied any discovery that his strict instructions were not followed.

On the other hand, my father—the seller in the company—was easygoing and fun, and worked equally as hard as Abe. He was always smiling, always handy with a joke or a friendly gesture. It was Poppa who could lay claim to Grandpa Solomon's legacy.

And it was obvious to me that his role in the family business was as important as Uncle Abe's, if not more so. Still, it troubled me because my uncle functioned as if he was the one and only boss and my father was the subordinate because he was younger. Whenever he could, my father calmed their conflicts with humor and outright appeals to brotherly love.

In Europe, Grandpa Solomon's shop was closed on Shabbat, but not so with our family in New York. We celebrated Shabbat with less ritual observances than the tradition in Poland, feeling just as comfortable as in our cultural history. Business was business, religion was religion, and there we were not traditional. They were two different things, and we were committed to both.

Saturdays usually meant less business. On that day, the floors were quiet. Tailors, cutters, and stock clerks were off. Lingering in the air was the familiar smell of burned cut cloth as it seeped from the cutting room factory into the office.

My father's office had a broad desk with a chair on the other side facing his, and a credenza behind the desk. The desk faced an alcove that overlooked Fifth Avenue. Off to the side were two leather nail-head armchairs with a small table and lamp in between. On the right was a coffee table with a trade newspaper. This was my poppa's choice of place to negotiate, tell a joke, and pour a drink for a customer at the office. It was his way of creating relationships that earned the trust of his customers.

As the result of a coin flip, Uncle Abe had the windowless office next to Poppa's, and he complained about it frequently. My uncle would monitor the staff of about fifteen from his doorway as they worked from high stools at huge tilted drafting tables bordered with a lip at the base to keep papers and drawing tools from slipping off.

A friend or acquaintance would often visit the shop to purchase a suit, coat, or sport jacket at wholesale price. Late in the summer, beautiful winter cashmere coats would arrive for early fall delivery to retailers throughout the city. In the autumn and winter, the racks sagged with new spring and summer suits, with more inventory in the warehouse. Saturdays brought motivated buyers, and on a good one, we could have a dozen customers.

This particular morning flew by. I was assigned to check the inventory and make records of sizes and quantities. About an hour before we planned to leave for home, two important-looking, well-dressed customers came into the showroom. Poppa instructed me to greet our visitors.

I stared at the older man from top to cuff. His silken white hair and alert eyes. His navy pinstriped suit, starch-pressed white shirt with cufflink sleeves. His silk paisley tie and matching pocket square. Clear-polished fingernails, and finally, impeccable shoes shined to a high gloss—a movie star, to all appearances. The younger man was more casually dressed in a blue blazer with silver buttons and gray slacks, but perfectly tailored to fit. In our line of business, it was only natural for me to appraise everyone's attire, well-dressed women included.

I offered my hand. "Good afternoon, gentlemen, I'm Haskell's son. My father has asked me to greet you. How can I be of help?" Without hesitating, I kept on: "May I show you some sample garments? I know you will love the quality and design. The fit is excellent." The words flew from my lips.

Both men cracked smiles. "You're a chip off the old block!" The older gentleman called to my father, "Hey, Haskell, your son is just like you—he started to sell us before he asked our names!" Everyone laughed.

Poppa gently turned to me. "Please ask our guests if they would like coffee, a glass of vaser [water], or whiskey." My father's gracious style, as I had been told, was much like my grandfather Solomon's, and cast a spell to put everyone at ease.

I felt pride, and only a touch of embarrassment as the white-haired gentleman called me to him.

"Please take my coat and my card." The card read, "Selwyn Slott, Men's Wear General Merchandise Manager & VP, Macy's 34th Street." The younger man's card also read that he was from Macy's: "Lawrence Hoyt, Men's Apparel Buyer." The look on their faces made plain who was sizing up who.

At seventeen, I understood the importance of these cards. But the wise guy in me turned to my father and said, "Poppa, I should also have business cards."

My father stared at me, then lifted his right arm, the back of his hand facing me. "You wanna smack?" His mock threat heralded a round of laughter.

The men sat at one of two green felt-covered tables and looked around our well-lit and tastefully designed showroom. They took in the comfortable brown leather chairs for customers and the immense garment closets on each end of the showroom, one containing samples for the current season and the other for past seasons.

It was time to work. My father held open a jacket for me as I tossed aside my own. He put one suit after another on my back as I became the fashion model for the moment. I opened the jacket buttons, showing the linings inside. I did a slow turn for our guests to appreciate the fit of the shoulders, how the fabric moved and fell against my frame exactly right.

Poppa draped the showroom table with sample garments like an artist working his canvas. He layered about fifty swatches in a pattern of crisscrosses, creating a dazzling display of hue and texture. I watched the two Macy executives become overwhelmed with the rainbow of color and cloth. They held swatches up to the light, feeling, rubbing, nodding to each other.

There followed a mile-a-minute detailed discussion of the potential best sellers, prices, delivery, fabric, and tailoring quality. I heard my father, the real boss of Abraham & Haskell as I saw it, stress the many advantages the company offered without stopping to take a breath.

"These fabrics are all imported worsted cloth and cashmere from Brazil, Mexico, and Canada. The tailoring quality, a number six grade—the best quality—is made in the USA, only one step below custom handsewn clothing." Poppa's sales pitch was not aggressive, yet it was nonstop, building to a climactic ending: "And now we offer to Macy's only—a new-added plus."

Both men smiled. My father returned their smile and paused so his final "sell" would have high impact. He said with confidence, "We are only ten minutes from your store, and will deliver all garments on hangers to Macy's Thirty-Fourth Street!"

Upon hearing the unique plus service, the Macy's executives turned to each other, nodded, and in unison said, "Done!"

With a flick of his hand, my father signaled to me to begin removing the swatches from the table and hanging the suits back in the sample closet. It was an exciting thirty-minute sales pitch, and I witnessed my father's expertise and talent. As my great-grandfather Moishe foresaw, his son Solomon would be one of the best clothing salespeople in the industry, and Grandpa Solomon passed his skills to my father. With luck, Dad would someday gift his skills to me.

Slott and Hoyt got up to leave the showroom. I was in the back of the shop. They called out to me, "Good-bye, Eric, nice to meet you." Their names tattooed into my memory, I ran back into the showroom and said, "Good-bye, Mr. Slott; good-bye, Mr. Hoyt!" We shook hands. When Poppa saw the expression of approval on his customers' faces, he beamed at me, and I drank in his pride.

It was close to four o'clock, late for a Saturday. My Uncle Abe and Cousin Melvin were gone. I was puzzled that Uncle Abe had not at least come into the showroom to say hello to these import-ant potential customers. *Uncle Abe's a strange person*, I thought, shaking my head.

On my father's desk lay a white envelope filled with crisp, new twenty-dollar bills. I had never seen so much cash in my life. Poppa counted the money, placed a twenty-dollar bill in my hand, and put the envelope into his inside breast pocket.

I felt I had arrived. I shut off the lights and locked the door. This new understanding of Poppa's talent and my own part in this success kept me warm in the eighteen-degree freezing weather as we walked to the subway station on our way home.

CHAPTER 8

THE RULES OF THE HOUSE

Haskell and Eric returned home after the Macy's buyers left. "Hi, Momma!" Eric called. "We're back from the shop!"

"Hello, hello!" she responded. "Hungry? I made cabbage soup and brisket." Mother was in the kitchen, moving from the sink to the stove and from the stove to the sink, busy with the evening's dinner.

"Sounds great, Momma. You know me, I'm always ready to eat." As he walked past her, he took the twenty-dollar bill from his pocket and placed it in her hand.

"What's this?" she exclaimed.

"It's the money I earned today."

She put her arms around him and pressed him to her bosom. "I love you!" she yelled [parental pride].

"Momma, let me breathe," Eric gasped.

"Shh, shh," she whispered. "I thank you. You are a good boy. Keep ten dollars and put ten in your bank account. Go wash up. We'll have supper soon."

Eric beamed and looked back over his shoulder as he walked away. "I love you back."

She looked at her son with her hand on her bosom.

Haskell stretched on his tiptoes as he reached for a bottle of whiskey in the upper kitchen cabinet, his favorite, Four Roses.

Looking over his shoulder, he poured a single drink into a shot glass, and in one swift motion, threw his head back and swallowed. A deep "aah" came from his gravelly voice. With eyes shut tight and shaking his head, he said to no one in particular, "I needed that."

He sat down at the kitchen table, contemplating his day. Macy's buyers, as well as the other few sales they made. Despite today's success, he still felt burdened.

Haskell had a strange feeling about his brother, and wondered why Abe was absent today, leaving him alone with Eric to meet with the Macy's buyers. Turning his head, Haskell noticed Eric standing nearby. "Use this time before supper to finish your home-work so you're ready for school on Monday."

"Can't I do it tomorrow? It's Saturday," Eric said in a half-moan, half-whine.

"Absolutely not! Be careful, my boy. You're walking on danger-ous waters when you talk to me like that."

Haskell, feeling a touch guilty, poured another whiskey. He could not completely accept any satisfaction for today's results. He carried a life sentence of guilt. His parents, Solomon and Hannah, had sent his older brothers, Label and Abraham, ahead two years before he had left. Label went to a farm cousin in Indiana. His parents had thought they were too old to immigrate, and Haskell's younger sister, Miriam, stayed to look after them. Trapped in Poland in 1939, they perished in the camps as Nazi evil infected Poland. The horror and permanent guilt Haskell felt for not insist-ing the entire family come to America never lifted from his psyche and permeated all issues that touched him on duty, work, and education, and always with respect. The family was haunted, the same as many other Jewish families. Which concentration camp? No one knew. Though not overtly religious, the Brodskys sat shiva, the Jewish mourning period, and contributed to a small synagogue in the neighborhood to honor their deceased family. The sense of falling short of one's responsibility was one of tragic proportions pervading their lives.

Haskell carried the burden of the generations of demanding work that demanded its due reward. This responsibility was his alone to execute and instruct to his children.

CHAPTER 9

HANNAHLA/ELLEN

Ellen, the eldest of the three Brodsky children, was determined not to be left out of the reinvention that America offered as her birthright. She was not to be overlooked. Born Hannah, referred to with affection as "Hannahla," she renamed herself "Ellen" to be more American, just as she called her father Dad instead of Poppa as her brothers did. She earned induction into Arista, the group of the highest achievers in grades and work ethic in her high school, and graduated second in her class, which made everyone proud.

On this night, in her late teens, Ellen—née Hannah, a.k.a. Hannahla—returned home from work simmering inside about her dull, horrible job as a secretary and file clerk in a garment center factory.

With the Brodsky work ethic flowing through her veins, she aspired to join her family company, only to find her father indifferent. She was livid. The traditions whereby sons were the only welcome partners while daughters were meant to marry, have babies, and be content with being wonderful homemakers enraged her.

Uncle Abe thwarted her ambition, unyielding in his insistence that they continue the historical tradition of employing sons only. For the sake of family peace, Haskell counseled his daughter, "Be patient, you must be patient, my Hannahla."

Ellen was not easygoing about this unfairness. She felt entitled to join the company as Uncle Abe's son had. She knew she was smarter and would work harder than her cousin Melvin. *That kid*, she thought, *what a jerk*.

Ely, the youngest of the three Brodsky children, was spending that evening with cousins. Still, Momma set the Friday night table like a stage for a full house. Tonight, the opening act was her cabbage soup, followed by her incomparable brisket and *tsimmes*, the roasted sweet potatoes and carrots that were her specialty. The finale featured the silver tea set and a scrumptious slice of home-made babka cake. Everyone piled Momma with their compliments as if afraid she might not continue to provide them with excellent meals. She loved dismissing them with a bashful wave. In truth, she valued the traditional gesture as superstition. She dodged these compliments to avoid a *keneinahora*, or evil eye, she dared not invite to her table.

The dinner conversation centered on Eric's academic work. They prodded him to explain his enthusiasm for French class, his sudden curiosity in math-related equations, and the problem he worked through in his chemistry course with success.

Ellen was pleased that Eric got center stage. She was preoccupied with other things.

To engage her daughter, Molly questioned, "How are things at work?"

Ellen made a face but said nothing.

"Hannah!" her father said sharply. "Momma asked you a question!"

He turned to his wife. "Molly, you should be firmer with your daughter!"

Ellen, who had been toying with her babka, looked up. "My name is Ellen, Dad! Sorry to complain, Momma, but I hate my job!"

Momma answered, "Don't say 'hate.'"

Ellen gave her a look and continued, "The people are stupid and uneducated. If we talk about the war and what's happening in the Pacific, it's like they live in a different world, and it's zero to them, as if nothing's happening, like they know nothing. Every week, we're visited by two scary-looking thugs who push our boss around until he passes them some money. They leer at all the girls, and it's frightening."

Ellen kept defending herself. "I'm not saying this is because anyone is an immigrant, I just don't want to be around goons, even if they only come once a week. So what if it seemed like a good lead from the high school placement office? What seemed like a good place to begin working, isn't.

"And Poppa, I am your daughter. You have my complete love and respect, yet you only think of the future for Eric and Ely and your old-world customs. I cherish your mother's name. It was a beautiful name for Poland, where you and she were born. I was born here, in America. I want an American name. Didn't you get a new name in America—Brodsky? How is this any different?"

Ellen was out of her chair now, pacing. "And one more thing, Poppa. I am quitting my job! I refuse to be held back one iota. I am not going to be left behind or left out of the action as your company's success grows. Imagine, if I were your son, your eldest child—is there any doubt that right now I would be working side by side with you? I am going to Uncle Abe and insisting that both of you find a place for me in the company. You wouldn't and shouldn't expect any less from me; I have your blood flowing through my veins, too!"

Haskell looked up, helpless at Ellen's outburst.

"There, that's settled!" she said.

"Bravo!" interjected Molly, as she slowly clapped her hands. Haskell saw she was as proud a mother as there ever was. He had no defense against them both. He raised his palms up as if to block more talk.

Ellen grabbed his palms and kissed them, as if he had agreed, which he hadn't. Not wanting to push her luck or break the spell, she crossed the room toward her bedroom, saying sweetly, "Good night, Momma. Good night, Poppa. I love you. Thanks for believing in me."

Molly sat there for a few minutes thinking through her own feelings and her daughter's. She knew it was time to voice her opinion in defense of Ellen, while understanding the battle that may come.

After clearing the table of the dishes and the Shabbat candles had burned down, she found herself facing Haskell in their bedroom. "Haskell, you are a good husband and a good father. We all live well because of your intelligence and hard work. I am proud to be Mrs. Brodsky. So, I know you will understand what I am about to say."

Haskell held up his hand, a gesture meaning he wanted to speak first. "What is on your mind?" she asked.

"Hannah said that she would not be held back one iota." Hesitatingly, he said, "What does 'iota' mean? I never heard such a word. What does it mean?" Molly pulled up a stool from the closet and sat across from him. "I could see that Hannah meant that nothing is going to stop her from joining your business. Not even the littlest speck, not anything. Like you, she is strong." Molly did not hesitate. "You are right to respect the memory of your mother. And no matter what Ellen calls herself, in your heart she will always have your mother's name. But you are mistaken to force your daughter to bear the name of your mother if it makes her unhappy.

"My husband, here you have a choice, and please listen carefully. If you can't tolerate the name she wants, you can decide: you either respect and love her, or you will lose her.

"You must value her needs as a young American woman. You and I are from traditional old-world customs, but the time has come to put those traditions aside, as difficult as that may be. We do not live in the ghetto of Poland anymore. A place where you and I, our friends and family, were all the same. Our language, religion, and how we lived. No one was different, and we all respected one another. We are in the New World, America."

Molly looked into Haskell's eyes, her hand tender on his cheek. "And please listen to me. Think this over carefully, for your own sake and happiness. You must be on her side and speak to Abe about giving Hannah a job at your shop. You have often told me that you and Abe are equal partners. If he has a child in the company, well, so should you."

Haskell thought, *She's right. We're not in Poland any longer. We're Americans. We're New Yorkers. She speaks true: no child is worth losing over a custom. I will do what Molly is suggesting. Stubborn though I am, I will surrender, God help me.*

"And one more thing," Molly said, "the American translation of 'Hannahla' is *Ellen*." She knew when enough was enough.

CHAPTER 10

MAY 1945, THE END OF WORLD WAR II

Molly was painfully aware that Eric was fast approaching the age when he would have to join the war effort. When she heard the long-awaited news over the radio—"Germans surrender unconditionally"—she could not contain herself, crying out, "Thank you, God!"

Eric and Ely came home from school to find their mother trembling and weeping with relief. Ellen returned elated from her office job. Haskell strode through the door, and they all rushed into his open arms in a heap of hugs and tears.

Eric, so close to draft age, took in the whole scene and soaked in the feelings of harmony, peace, and safety. For the moment, they all pushed thoughts of the continuing war with Japan out of their minds.

Newspaper headlines and radio broadcasts repeated: "General Eisenhower Extracts"; "Unconditional Surrender from Germany." Relief and joy reverberated throughout the country. Celebrations broke out in every city, town, and village. In places like New York, the streets were borderline bedlam with crowds marching and shouting and kissing each other with abandon. It was a moment in history to salute, memorialize, and celebrate.

In the Brodskys' neighborhood, a woman sat rocking back and forth alone on her porch, her arms wrapped tightly around her body. A neighbor called out, "Mrs. Weinstein, why so sad? This is a joyful day!" She leveled her gaze at him and spoke slowly, "For you, it is. For me, my son will never come home."

Remorse and pain for the bereaved dimmed the rejoicing. The war continued in Japan.

Abraham & Haskell's shop closed for two days after the victory. On the third day, Haskell could see the end of the war with Japan was in sight. The time was ripe for unprecedented business growth. Unlike his competitors, Haskell had prepared for this moment by stockpiling materials and supplies. He reinforced his labor team and assembled ample machinery, especially for womens wear to accommodate the newly expanded female workforce. As he sat at his desk above the sounds of street celebrations, he concentrated on launching this postwar endeavor. His plan meant juggling an audacious sales approach with a realistic strategy that could compensate for any contingencies.

He dialed his Macy's friend at the store's corporate offices. The voice answered plainly, "Selwyn Slott."

"Good morning, Selwyn, and mazel tov to all of us! Thank God, soon your son will return home!" Haskell hoped there had not been sad news about Selwyn's soldier son.

Slott watched the throngs in Herald Square celebrating below his window, but he was too preoccupied to celebrate without reservation. He reflected on his options and decided to be frank with Haskell.

"Our son is safe, thank God. At the same time, I despise myself for not fully giving my heart over to celebrating. Part of me will not allow me to enjoy this moment as I should. My conscience is choking me. I cannot stand who I have become."

In the oppressive silence that followed, Haskell thought he could hear Selwyn suffocating with embarrassment. "Selwyn, let me assure you that you may speak to me in confidence," he said. "Tell me what bothers you, my friend. Please, tell me," Haskell pleaded.

"Promise not to tell this to anyone, not to Abe, not to your wife, not to anyone," Slott begged.

"I pledge you can trust me," Haskell vowed.

"Since the German surrender and the elation and happiness of the world just three days ago, I thought we would have a bursting of pent-up demand and a crush of shoppers. But the store is almost empty. Business is miserable! All I see are people outside dancing and singing, kissing, enjoying themselves. I am ashamed that all I can think about is business. Is this the end or the beginning? It's all I ever think about. Is it good for business? Is it bad for business? Is our business up or down? So I was sitting here, ashamed, when you called. Is peace good for business? Because now business is terrible."

Haskell sat there, stunned. *What a shmuck! I thought he had cancer! Is it only business? He is worse than my brother Abe, thinking about nothing but money!*

He drew a deep breath and patiently replied, "Selwyn, I know you like a book. What you are going through is not a terrible thing. So what, you are a businessman and it consumes your life. Today is your lucky day! Your worries are over! Cheer up! I am your guardian angel. In thirty seconds, when you hear my plan, you will be your old happy self."

"I doubt it. What are you selling today that I cannot and will not buy?"

Haskell was glad that Selwyn couldn't see the grin on his face. He stood up and leaned back against his desk. "Mr. Slott, are you sitting or standing?"

"I am sitting."

"My dear friend, stand up! We are on the cusp of the future! This is not the time to think; it is the time to act! A wave of tens of thousands of young men and women—no, change that to hundreds of thousands of people—will be returning home from overseas and flooding your store because they will all need suits, shirts, ties, shoes, and underwear. They will need *everything*. How can you just sit there? Can you afford to miss the opportunity to fill your store with everything our young heroes need? With your instincts for new opportunities at the helm, you will make more inroads in the next five years than in any prior five, or even ten. This uncontainable demand is what you have wanted your whole career." My father took a breath and sipped some water from a glass near his phone.

Selwyn listened. "Go on, go on."

"Our company has foreseen that the postwar demand for civilian clothing will be going through the roof. We propose that we be a key link in your supply chain to quench this new level of customers' needs. We can and will beat the competition to help you meet the unleashed hunger coming soon. With your backing, we are ready to activate our extended network and order cloth from every worthwhile manufacturer here in the US, Mexico, Canada, and South America. The moment that commerce in Europe begins to stir back to life, our company will be their first and best American customer from the trade. We have built and maintained a workforce and supply chain of everything, from fabric to notions, and we can produce what you will need.

"What your store needs is a partner. I want—I insist—right now that you place orders with us for five thousand men's suits and five thousand sport jackets, as well as ten thousand pairs of trousers. For women, I suggest two thousand dresses, one thousand blouses, one thousand skirts, and five hundred pairs of trousers. Don't waste a moment! Macy's will be the *only* shop in New York— no, the *only* shop in the United States—able to dress every man and woman for the next two years. Others will only promise. We will fulfill."

Haskell leaned forward on his desk. "In the past three months, during our mutual business, we have not even broken a sweat as we have fulfilled your orders one hundred percent. You have seen our factory, our facilities, our skilled workers. And we have accrued capital for this expansion. Listen to me. I want you to promise to keep my confidence, too: I, too, live and breathe business. So, we understand each other. Now, I am making you this exclusive offer. What do you think?"

After a pause, Selwyn audibly exhaled. "Haskell, thank you for your perspective. It will be a *seller's* market, for a change. I need to move on securing our supply before our competitors do. Would you do me a favor?"

"We trust each other. We are not just friends; we are partners," Haskell said smoothly.

"Macy's must have priority. Give us an exclusive for a week; don't make this offer to our competitors until we decide. If I get the OK from management, I want us to have a head start for the best of what you have. I will let you know our decision as soon as possible."

"Selwyn, listen to me, fuck management. You are our best customer. Go to the owners of Macy's. I will promise you on one condition. You must get back to me within the week. Macy's sets the pace, now you must dress the peace."

Selwyn laughed. "How can I resist? Get me your proposal today in writing."

Haskell had the prewritten proposal on Selwyn's desk that afternoon, but added to the agreement, "Macy's must pay Abraham & Haskell a one-third deposit to be able to finance this project."

Selwyn called to say it would be seriously considered within the week. Haskell indulged himself, imagining the nods of approval this would have elicited from his father, Solomon, his grandfather Moishe, and his great-grandfather Havrohm.

At the end of the week, Selwyn called to inform Haskell that Macy's had placed the order. He instructed Haskell to submit an invoice for one-third as deposit for the order.

Haskell rewarded himself by indulging in the arc of his own success. How far he had come from a sewing machine in his family's nineteenth-century Polish tailor shop to supplying New York's largest department store! *My grandfather Moishe and my father, Solomon, would be so proud.*

When the postman delivered the Macy's order in a certified letter, Haskell gazed at the order in wonderment, as if it were Excalibur. He even considered framing it. He knew the import of this moment, and even imagined it in his eulogy: "In the family business's fourth generation, Haskell laid the groundwork for a dramatic expansion that honored the legacy of hard work by his ancestors."

Holding the unthinkable, unbelievable order in his hands spurred Haskell to waste no time in extending the initiative with Macy's to other companies. To hook even two or three other major department stores would be a huge accomplishment.

Invigorated, he called Molly to share the good news. He spent the afternoon pitching to his connections at Wanamaker's Department Store in Philadelphia, Shillito's in Cincinnati, Goldsmith's in Memphis, and Sears & Roebuck in Chicago. He telephoned the presidents at Howard Clothes and Crawford's Men's Wear in New York. He planned to contact the JCPenney executive office in New York City and the new store that had recently opened on Union Square, called Klein's on the Square. He made a mental note to call Nordstrom on the West Coast in a few hours. With each executive, Haskell perfected the script. It helped that Selwyn said he could cite Macy's order (but not the terms) to stimulate other retailers. He thought, *Success breeds success.* He never forgot the commitment to Selwyn that Macy's would always be first.

In the giddiness of the day, he came to think that their factory and office on Fifth Avenue were becoming too small and the staff inadequate.

CHAPTER 11

A DAUGHTER'S LOVE

June was a busy month. It was not that Haskell wouldn't want to speak to his daughter at any time, but work was work, and nobody called him if it wasn't imperative. Also, telephone calls cost money. Sometimes, when a family member went home, they called and let it ring, advising them they'd arrived safely; if you didn't answer, you weren't charged for the call.

His secretary was busy on the other line, so Haskell answered the phone with his customary, "Hello, Abraham & Haskell, Men's Clothing."

"Dad, it's me, Ellen."

"Hannahla, darling, how are you?"

"It's *Ellen.* I'm good."

"Is there anything special on your mind?"

"Nothing important. I just wanted to start the week by calling to say hello and I love you."

"I love you back, darling. You must be very rich to call just to say hello, *Ellen*," Haskell said.

"I have a wealthy father. Also, I'm calling you from my job, so, gotta go! Love you! Bye!"

His daughter's sweet voice was worth any interruption or distraction, and he was hearing it increasingly since taking Molly's advice to address her as Ellen. A telephone call like this was his ample reward. Haskell congratulated himself with the thought, *A rich man could not hope for better, for what is wealth but to enjoy such love and devotion.*

CHAPTER 12

THE WAR ENDS

August 1945. World War II was ending. My father and I, alone in his men's clothing factory, scanned the fifty racks of men's suits and sport jackets manufactured for the fall/winter season. He stood in silence, looking, shaking his head, stroking his chin, considering his plan for the sale of every garment. He didn't appear concerned; he was planning his strategy.

In this silence, rare for Poppa, he turned to me and began one of his many Yuboroffsky family accounts. I devoured every word. I honored his description of our family's lives, loves, and fears. I reveled in each incident and struggled to remember every word, every moment. As I got older, it occurred to me: our history, generation after generation, translated its own record of experiences, all with slight changes and minor exaggerations. Thus, each anecdote was embellished, becoming more interesting. Each proud elder grandfather passed his legend to his eldest son and the next son and the next son and to me, the great-great grandson of Havrohm.

Poppa sighed. "You know, Eric, as time has passed, I have seen the world has changed. We have been lucky. I look back and see that the Yuboroffsky women have had their own powerful work ethic and intuitive knowledge of life, of love and loss. They may have been undervalued." He took a step and ran a hand over the shoulder of one of the suits.

"Our brides became the influence and the leaders of the family and its business." He shrugged. "Women are the true power of life. We as men merely fulfill our dreams if we are lucky with the right choices we make as men. The most important and truly our most valuable choice in life is the woman we persuade to be our wife."

CHAPTER 13

Eric, sitting in a phone booth, called his father and asked, "Poppa, I just left school, it's only a half day for the teachers to prepare our final exams. How about taking me to lunch? It's almost twelve thirty."

Haskell smiled, hearing his son's voice. "OK, where do you want to go?"

"Let's go for pizza. It's two blocks away from the office."

Haskell was taken aback. "Pizza? Are you eating traif [non-kosher food]?"

"Poppa, it's dairy—only cheese and tomato sauce on a large piece of bread, so no problem. Try it—you'll love it. I will meet you in front of the office in ten minutes."

It was a spectacular New York City day—a touch cool in the shade, warm in the sun. Together, Haskell and his son strode two avenues along Fourteenth Street, delighting in the sight of crowds still in the streets celebrating the victory of World War II, including the drunk, the half-undressed, and the exhausted with nowhere better to go. The most outrageous of these was a topless, laughing woman. Father and son cast each other sideways glances and stifled their grins.

A right turn at Union Square brought them to the sign reading "Gina's Homemade Pizza." Inside, the restaurant was festive, noisy, and crowded. Haskell stiffened. Other patrons were clearly eating pizza with cheese . . . and ham. Not kosher. Haskell shut his eyes and clenched his teeth. "I cannot eat here. Let's go."

"Poppa, please, try it. It's not what you think. Let's order a simple pizza, cheese and tomato. Take one bite, and if you hate it, spit it out and we will leave. OK? Please?"

Haskell did not consent or refuse. He remained silent. *Oy vey. My son—he's going to be a great seller!*

At the table next to theirs, an elderly couple insisted on sharing their wine. Eric declined, saying, "I'm only seventeen!" But he implored Haskell, "Have some, Poppa! It's a true yontif [holiday]!" A small gesture brought a fist-sized fluted glass that was immediately filled. They toasted in unison, "To life!" to which the elderly man added, "and peace in the world!" They drank that small glass together, the couple stood, and in an old-world enactment, leaned slightly forward from their waists in an almost imperceptible bow as they departed.

Eric ordered a small plain pizza, well done, a Coke for himself, and a 7UP for his father. The waitress served a flat pan of what looked like thick matzo spread with red sauce and white cheese to their table. Eric pantomimed formality as he served his father a slice of the pie.

"It smells good," Poppa said, surprised.

"Take a bite," Eric pleaded.

Haskell closed his eyes and lifted it to his lips. For a moment, the smell took him back, the garlic taste and aroma of his mother's cooking. He shook the nostalgia off and gave in to his son's plea. He bit down. It was good, particularly good. "Oy vey!" He was going to have to admit it. *Our new country, every day always new things in America. Always new things in this wonderful America.*

Still, trying not to sound too enthusiastic, Haskell underplayed it. "Very good. And what do you call this?"

"Pizza, Poppa, pizza! I told you, it's delicious. And, get this, I know it matters to you and Momma—it's pareve [neutral food]!"

"Maybe I'll try another piece." This is how, on occasion, Haskell coddled his son, by allowing him to be right.

Eric's reward was simply sitting next to his father, pleased and proud. He was his own hero.

At last, after two decades in America, to finally try pizza. Haskell thought, *This experiment, eating pizza, was my most major step to . . .* His reverie was interrupted when a woman approached their table. She spoke with an Italian accent, struggling to sound more American. "It's good to see you again. Where is your cousin, Melvin?"

"Oh, I'm not sure." Eric looked away, then back to the woman. "This is my father, Haskell Brodsky."

"Ah, Mr. Brodsky, nice to meet you. My name is Gina. Welcome to our kitchen."

Haskell stood and bowed his head respectfully, putting his hand forward in a friendly handshake and gazing into the woman's eyes.

Gina continued, "You have such a good son. He keeps to himself and is always polite and proper. You did an excellent job."

"Blame his mother for the good job," Haskell quipped, smiling.

She was more serious. "No, no, it takes both a momma and a poppa to raise a son. Then she called her son. "Anthony! Come and meet Eric's father."

Anthony was a skinny boy, taller than Eric, warm and friendly. "It's very nice to meet you, Mr. Brodsky." He extended his hand politely.

Haskell said to Anthony, "I see that you work in the family business. Is your father here, too?"

Anthony was frank. "My father passed away. He never worked here. He did other things. It's my mom's shop, but it's not my intention to work here forever. Part of the reason I am working is to make enough money so that I can visit your factory. Eric invited me to buy a suit wholesale for my prom and for when I go on job interviews after graduation."

With an approving glance, Haskell looked at the boy, replying graciously, "Please come anytime."

"There's a chance I may not make it. The prom is the first week of June and here it is, May eleventh."

"I insist you come anyway, *before* your prom. We will give you a special price for a boy who has a beautiful mother and makes such delicious . . . *what* do you call it?" Haskell turned slightly to his son as he pretended to forget.

"Pizza, Poppa, pizza!"

Haskell winked at his son. "Let's go. We have some work to do." He sipped the last of his 7UP through a straw, retrieved two dollars from his pocket, and placed it on the table.

"No, please!" Gina's smile was warm, her eyes twinkling. "It is my treat."

He nodded and thanked her, and steadfastly deflected her entreaties to take back the tip. He wouldn't think of not leaving it on the table. He pleased himself, thinking, *Could it be that the pizza has made me a true American? New country, new things.*

CHAPTER 14

THE QUARREL

Aslew of orders from retailers throughout the country followed. The usually reliable Abe had not shown up to work and had not advised anyone as to why not.

"Where is your father?" Haskell asked Melvin. The boy shrugged.

Abe not at the office? How could that be? Haskell knew that business was always Abe's primary focus; it was his brother's silent commitment as well as his own. If either Abe or Haskell were not planning to come to work, advising each other was necessary.

Abe's absence troubled Haskell. It was unusual, and Haskell remembered Abe had also missed the meeting with the Macy's buyers. This was a serious matter that had to be addressed soon; he was not a man who allowed an unsolved issue to fester. He would give it one more day.

The next morning, Abe arrived at the office, unshaven and disheveled. Haskell was taken aback. Neither exchanged hellos. Haskell followed Abe into his office as the lights flooded the dark room. Normally neat, the office, too, was disheveled. Haskell's gaze registered the papers strewn about, both the cash receivable and payable books lying carelessly on the floor under the window.

Haskell took his seat squarely opposite his brother. "You look like dreck [crap]—are you sick?"

Abe remained silent. He didn't look up from reading letters and invoices one by one, placing them down in three orderly stacks.

Haskell got up and left, saying flatly, "I'm in my office if you want to talk."

Time passed and he thought Abe would come to his office and talk. He didn't.

Haskell survived the stretch of the day, waiting for Abe to make the overture, but he didn't. Abe needed to step forward. This standoff couldn't continue. The time had come to clear the air.

Abe knew this as well. He hesitated at the door of Haskell's office before he entered. "Haskell, I have a confession," he said.

Haskell looked up from his papers, his voice cool and composed. "I'm waiting to hear. You made me wait. You know I hate it when we fight or argue, but it is past time for us to talk. I am disappointed in you." He let the word "disappointed" hang in the air like a formal accusation.

"I can understand," Abe said, mimicking Haskell's even tone, attempting to appear casual. "I borrowed money for a side investment without consulting you."

At first, Haskell didn't respond. He stood up and straightened his back, holding back his anger. He leveled his accusation, served directly with a glare: "You took five thousand dollars out of our account without telling me, and there is no record of what it was for. You had no right to do that. You think you're the older, smarter brother and I am still a kid. When we got in this business, our agreement was we were equal partners. That was our pact when we began. We shook on it. You gave me your word."

Haskell saw his brother's face pale. He did not have the patience for a long, convoluted explanation. He spun the accounts ledger across the desk to Abe.

His eyes burning, Haskell let loose with resentments brewing since childhood: "And any advantage you ever had being two years my senior has expired! You are done underestimating me!" In his gut, Haskell knew there could be no reasonable explanation for what Abe had done. Their discussion stalled, and the tension in the room crackled.

Abe's face fell, his confidence crushed by the pain and anger in Haskell's voice.

Abe stammered his way through a futile quest to defuse the issue. "We have made a wise investment with the Levy Brothers in the banking business. It will bring an exceptionally good return for us."

Haskell had heard talk that these arrangements were always dangerous. He could not hold back, even though his inner voice cautioned him: *Do not humiliate your brother.*

Haskell was having none of it. He roared as his anger burst. "Are you telling me you gave our five thousand dollars to the three Levy brothers? They are shylocks—more Mafia than the Mafia! Everyone in our neighborhood knows who they are! *Thugs!* You will never see any interest or a single cent of *your* investment."

By now Haskell was pacing, glaring at Abe. "Trust me, Abe. The money is gone."

Abe tried to continue. "The Levys have always been successful. What are you talking about?"

"Abe. Everyone knows who the Levys are. How did you miss that? How could you be so naive?"

Abe looked shocked, embarrassed.

Haskell could almost hear his father's voice as he continued lacerating his brother. He knew Abe heard it, too. Haskell fought to hold back an anger greater than he had ever felt toward his brother.

"You gave the Levys five thousand, and they will give you sixty-five/thirty-five split of the earnings, am I correct? You put up all the money and you get a minority portion of the profits, right?"

Abe hung his head while Haskell continued to badger him.

"And you are supposed to be a smart businessman? In *this* shop, here in *this* office, *we* invest one hundred percent of the money. And *we* get ninety-three percent of the gross. *Our* salesmen get seven percent commission. *You* are the major investor, and *they* are the sellers, right?"

In the silence building between them, Haskell calmed. He came around his desk to face his brother. He put his arm around Abe's shoulders, his voice more natural. "Are you so hungry to get rich quick? There is no such thing! The only thing that brings in money is hard work, superior quality, and taking care of our customers."

With Haskell's simple analysis, Abe's shoulders collapsed. But he found his voice. Into silence, Abe spoke: "I will try to get our money back Monday. I am sorry. It was a big mistake. I should have spoken to you first. It will never happen again."

The confrontation had forced long-simmering issues into the open, and at that moment, every firmament of their world inverted. Haskell assumed the senior role; his brother Abe became relegated to a lesser position.

With Abe's capitulation, the end of the old and the beginning of the new came into sight. Haskell's release brought him back to his senses. Recognizing his brother was neck-deep in disgrace, he softened inside. *Oy vey. I feel awful for him. I need to ease up. He feels ashamed for his error.*

Abe searched his brother's expression for any trace of sympathy. He wasn't sure he saw it. He recognized the cold glint in Haskell's eyes dissolving into a forgiving acknowledgment of fraternity, adding a sharper edge to his deepening pain.

"I am going to fix this," Abe vowed. "I will."

CHAPTER 15

THE PAYBACK

A few days later, Haskell was in his office, mulling over his confrontation with Abe, when the telephone rang.

"Hello, Haskell Brodsky speaking."

"Haskell, it's Ida!" she screamed. "Abe is in St. Vincent's Hospital. He had a heart attack."

"I'm coming right over!" Haskell said. *Oy vey, oy vey, what did I do? I was too tough on him. Please God, save him. I'm so sorry. I love him. I was too angry about him going to those shysters. This must be connected. His wife will never forgive me. God may not forgive me. I may never forgive myself.*

The hospital was close: over two avenues and down three streets. Running was the best option. With every step, he berated himself for his harsh words with Abe. Haskell ran as fast as he could, whispering a prayer, *Please don't let me have a heart attack, too.*

A physician was listening to Abe's heart when Haskell burst into the hospital room, and when he saw Haskell, he pulled the stethoscope away from Abe's chest as Ida introduced them.

"Doctor, what do you know?" Haskell asked.

"Abe was found collapsed on Rivington Street," the doctor said. "Fortunately, only a quarter hour passed between his discovery on the sidewalk and when the ambulance rushed him to the hospital. They could not yet determine if the bruises on his face and body came from the fall or from a mugging attack." The doctor checked the oxygen tube in Abe's nose, the intravenous tube going into his arm, and the tube that led under the sheet.

Haskell's head pounded with guilt and questions. *Why did he have several deep bruises around his head, a large cut on his jaw, and a bandage wrapped around his arm? Could that have happened in a fall during a heart attack?*

Ida sat nearby, moaning and trembling, clasping and wringing her hands. The doctor shot Haskell in a look, and Haskell walked to Ida to calm her. She tugged at him "Oy, Haskell, what was my Abe doing on Rivington Street? Such a bad neighborhood! The past few months, he's been meshuga [insane], not the same Abe I married. When I ask, he just says 'business'—what business is it? Is he mixed up in something bad?"

Before Haskell could answer, the sound of an alarm from one of Abe's machines riveted their attention to the bed. The doctor yelled, "Nurse!"

In a surreal flurry of motion that appeared both frantic and in slow motion, they watched the frenzied effort to save Abe. Suddenly they stopped, and all the helpful faces turned pale. As they stood back from the bed, heads bowed, the doctor turned to Ida and Haskell.

"I'm sorry."

Haskell thought he saw Ida almost will her own life to leave her body as if to follow her husband's. Haskell gathered up his sister-in-law so she would not swoon to the floor.

CHAPTER 16

THE FUNERAL AND SHIVA

Abe's funeral was held within three days according to Jewish tradition. Our family sat shiva [mourning], coming together in a show of unity as friends and relatives offered their support and respect. For a week, a procession of family and friends from every city and state came to pay their respects, including their brother Label from Indiana.

A condolence call from Selwyn Slott and Lawrence Hoyt from Macy's was a level of deference Haskell did not expect. He recognized their expression of sympathy was sincere and the significance of their partnership on the verge of this new era.

Condolence calls came in from representatives of other retailers he had written to (and were not customers yet) as well as three merchandisers from JCPenney.

In a moment of guilt and confusion, Haskell slapped the side of his head. He shut his eyes in pain, full of shame. *Here I am, my brother just died. And I cannot control my thoughts about business. It's all I think about. Tell me, God, am I a bad person? I bear all the guilt for trying to outshine the dreams that my ancestors Solomon, Moishe, and Havrohm had for themselves and our family legacy.*

On the second evening of the seven-day mourning period, Haskell tugged Eric into a room alone, and whispered, "I want you to go to the shop and see what is going on. Pretend you are me;

I want you to be the boss. Ask Paul, our foreman, how things are going. Look at the mail. Let me know if there is anything important. See if any checks have come and inform Mr. Aronson, our accountant. He keeps records and makes deposits. Don't stay too long. I need you back here to help with Aunt Ida and Melvin and the family."

Sitting shiva was a solemn time for reverence and reflection. Still, Haskell ran through scenarios of what had happened when Abe went to the Levy brothers' office to get back their $5,000. He could see what had happened in his mind's eye. He saw Abe walk right into their office. Haskell heard his brother's voice, "Morris, is Heshy in the office today?" Abe's voice would have been aggressive.

"No, what's up, something wrong?"

"I thought it over. My brother is against it; I want my money back." Abe's voice would have been growing louder, his eyes more intense.

"Are you nuts? What the fuck are you screaming about? The money is on the street. Two days ago!"

"What do you mean, it's on the street?"

"We made the loans, and you will get your share."

"You keep the interest; just give me the money back."

Knowing his brother's temper, the argument with Morris would have escalated. Haskell imagined Abe grabbing Morris's collar, shoving him, and threatening to go to the police, thinking this tepid show of force would impress Morris. Haskell knew it would not. He could see Morris smashing a bottle across Abe's head, as Abe would make an easy target, unlikely to dodge the swing.

"Listen to me, you stupid asshole, you ever threaten our family with the police again, I will fucking kill you!" Morris would have considered it an act of mercy to take Abe by his collar and drag him out without giving him a worse beating.

This scene played out in Haskell's mind as he sat quietly during his mourning. At the same moment, a cascade of guilt and remorse coursed through him. *Oh, Abe, you might be alive today if you weren't so strong-headed and thin-skinned, if you had not spent your life allowing your anger to overrule your common sense. No one wins with anger! God, please forgive me. While I spent the last month congratulating myself for my material success, I failed to protect my brother.*

Haskell sat bent on his low stool, his face in his hands. *I should have gone with him. If I had, I could have prevented this. There was no reason I shouldn't have gone, but I was preoccupied with greed, the vanity of success, wallowing in pride about how my grandfather Solomon would be proud of me while I forgot the ancient words of Solomon in Ecclesiastes: "Vanity of vanity; all is vanity chasing the wind."*

Haskell allowed himself to weep and became more deeply ashamed that those around him presumed he was crying for his brother. He twisted in pain. *I have failed. I have failed Abe. I have failed my family.*

CHAPTER 17

THE TURNING OF THE SCREW

Eric returned home from the shop at five o'clock. He had been there since noon. "Poppa, I spoke to Paul; he sends his condolences to the family. I also found three checks for payments made by customers. I called Mr. Aronson."

"How much?" his father asked. Eric pulled a little paper from his pocket and said, "Fourteen thousand, four hundred and eight-seven dollars."

Eric explained how he tried to carry himself with dignity befitting the occasion, understanding that his presence signaled the first family appearance post-Abe. He knew that even as a teenager, he wouldn't want to come across as presuming to be the new heir apparent. He made a conscious effort to be humble as he greeted those in the shop, hearing their individual condolences. He continued with ordinary tasks, watched the production on the cutting table, checked progress in the tailor room, and looked into the sample closets.

"And Poppa, I brought you letters from companies I've never heard you mention."

"Who were they?" Haskell asked eagerly.

Eric reached into the breast pocket of his jacket, pulled out four envelopes, and put them in his father's hand.

Haskell looked at them as if they were treasure maps: the first was from Sears & Roebuck, Chicago, the next from Shillito's, Cincinnati, and the third from Abe Stark, a high-end Brooklyn shop on Pitkin Avenue. The last was the biggest surprise of all, Nordstrom. A fine Seattle department store founded in 1901.

• • •

The shiva was over. Haskell returned to work, catching up with the production team and taking accounting meetings in person and by telephone. Amid the clutter that had accumulated during the past week, he caught sight of an envelope diagonally tucked underneath a pile of documents. The back was sealed, and when he turned it over, he recognized Abe's handwriting across the front.

To Haskell.

He held the envelope gently, taking a deep breath. He carefully opened the letter and read in silence:

Dear Haskell,

I am deeply sorry I made this terrible mistake, taking money without consulting with you. I wanted to make an investment that would bring cash into the company. Everyone thinks that I am the smart one. How wrong they are. You, my young brother, are blessed with all the talent that I always wanted for myself. Everyone loves you; your gift is that you love people.

I am going to Levy's this afternoon to get our money back and return it to our business. I will offer that they keep all the profits. It should work. Don't worry.

Abe

Haskell felt the weight of Cain and Abel, Jacob and Esau, and now, his own guilt at Abe's death. He wasn't sure if his tears were for Abe or himself. Waves of shame and self-loathing consumed him. *I caused my brother's death; I will never forgive myself.*

Gagging on his own mucus and saliva, he spit into the trash can beside his desk then scrambled to his feet as if God himself was bearing down on him and he *davened* [prayed] his manic prayers beseeching relief.

He felt his invocations were coming up short, and that the moment of remorse called for more. He had to be more honest than he had ever been in his life. He knew he owed the authentic confession in his own words, not the prayers of those who came before him. He felt himself called to account for his role in his brother's death.

Standing as if in obedience to the presence of the Almighty, Haskell shook off his normal equivocations to gain the strength to make core admission of his faults: *I brought this heartache on to myself, on Abe, on Ida, on my family. I bullied him and I put money before family because I am greedy and prideful.* Yet hard on the heels of his moments of penance, he could not shake the urge to blame Abe, the Levys, and anyone else.

Enough self-pity! I, too, am a victim of this. Who knows what fallout awaits.

He pulled himself together and remembered where he was as his secretary announced, "Mr. Brodsky, there is a young man to see you." He removed his skullcap and rubbed the tears from his eyes as he walked from his office.

"Excuse me, I have a slight cold," he said to the young man waiting. "How can I help you?"

The young man paused and looked closely at Haskell's face. "If it's a bad time, I can return tomorrow or the next day."

"No, no," Brodsky responded politely. "Please, tell me, to what do I owe your visit?"

"I am Anthony, Gina's son from the pizza restaurant. I hope you recall, we met a few days ago and you said that I could visit and buy a suit for my prom that's coming up."

"Yes, I do remember." Haskell turned to his supervisor. "Paul, show this young man some of our suits from the spring collection. Send him back here to me for the price."

In less than an hour, Paul and Anthony knocked on Haskell's door. He waved them in and examined the young man's selection, a blue blazer and light gray pair of pants.

Haskell's generous heart knew that because the boy had no father to help him, he had never learned about dressing for special occasions.

He took a breath and spoke softly. "Anthony, this is not what you should wear to a prom. My suggestion would be a dark blue suit over a white shirt and a blue tie. I am only guessing, but I think your date will be wearing a gown."

Anthony smiled and nodded his agreement. Haskell turned to Paul. "Bring me style number fifty-four hundred in a size thirty-seven long."

Anthony saw the navy suit Paul produced, and he knew Mr. Brodsky was right, but he hesitated.

Haskell caught his look and asked, "How much money do you have?"

"I have thirty-eight dollars."

"Paul, invite Anthony to the tailor shop to fix him up. Cuffs and sleeve alteration. Get everything done by tomorrow morning. The price for your new graduation prom suit will be nineteen dollars. You are going to need the rest for your prom date. Go."

Paul smiled at Haskell, and with a nod acknowledged this generosity as he had many times before.

Anthony shifted as he stood, stunned by his good luck. "This is really a gift, and no offense, I don't know if my mother will let me accept it without paying more, Mr. Brodsky."

"Tell your mother that we are going to eat your pizza forever!"

Smiles filled the room, and Anthony gave Haskell a gaze of sincere appreciation. "Thank you, Mr. Brodsky. Thank you."

Haskell placed his hand on the young man's shoulder. "Go, go. Have a fun time. Congratulations."

CHAPTER 18

THE ITALIAN AND JEWISH MAFIA FAMILIES MEET

The hushed room contrasted with the neighborhood's tumult outside: squealing bus brakes, honking cars, the clanging of the Delancey Street trolley, the shouts of mothers overseeing their children playing, a hawking peddler selling sour pickles from a barrel.

In the smoke-filled room, five men sat around the minyan table for ten. Heshy Levy was the eldest of his two brothers Tevye and Morris, whose cigarette dangled from his lips. At the far end sat Salvatore Santini and Carlo Tucci. Carlo's younger brother, Dino, stood silently with both hands in his pockets.

Heshy turned to Sal, a tinge of fear in his voice. "Listen, it was not us. He was a nice Jewish guy. He was one of us, an investor, looking to make a quick buck. He came to us."

Heshy's hand trembled ever so slightly. "We never knew, I swear on my mother, we never knew him. That's the truth."

Sal kicked his chair back as he stood up, "Mario told you the rules. You take the Jews. The Italians and the Pollacks are ours! The split is eighteen percent of the take and you keep the rest. We protect you. I remember the meeting. I was there. It was truly clear, and there could be no mistake."

Sal turned to Morris. "Put that fuckin' cigarette out. It'll kill you." At the mention of his name and the word "kill," the young brother stamped out his cigarette in a panic.

Satisfied he'd had the desired effect, Sal sat back down and continued, "We made the deal—we all agreed—there was to be no rough stuff unless Mario gave the OK. You guys have fucked up, and bad."

"The guy threatened to go to the police!" blurted Morris.

"Damn it! Shut your mouth!" Heshy commanded.

Sal's lips pressed together into a menacing line across his face. "I don't want anyone coming to me or Mario asking us questions or snooping around. You assholes better fix this and fast, or we will."

Sal turned to Carlo. "Let's get the fuck outta here. I told Mario when he made this deal that these guys would be nuttin' but trouble."

Heshy got up and approached Sal with his hand extended but pulled it back slowly when Sal did not extend his own. He tried another approach. "Hey, Sal, what's the big deal? So, the old guy got skittish, he got a few bangs, there was no harm. That's not rough stuff."

Sal stared straight into Heshy's face. "Ya know, Heshy, there's this dumb rumor I hear in our neighborhood that you Jew boys are supposed to be smart. Is that right? Well, the guy you roughed up. Abe Brodsky?"

"Yeah?" Heshy tried to be nonchalant as he tried to figure out how Sal got Abe's name. "So?"

"He croaked."

All three, Sal, Dino, and Carlo, spat on the floor. Carlo got in his first, only, and the last word.

"Your assholes are in big trouble."

With that, they swept out, slamming the door behind them.

CHAPTER 19

THE FUTURE COMES INTO FOCUS

In the period after the German and Japanese surrenders, success settled on the Brodskys' business, and their growth exceeded their wildest dreams. The sales formula Haskell pitched to his clients produced orders for thousands of men's suits, coats, and trousers. Women's clothing orders increased as much. Sales climbed to over $2 million. Every retailer among Brodsky's clients anticipated the return of hundreds of thousands of veterans. Haskell's Midas touch bestowed a bonanza upon the Brodsky family.

The following March, Molly arranged a family-only party celebrating Poppa's fifty-second birthday. The happy event took place at Hammer's kosher restaurant on Manhattan's Union Square, two blocks from the shop. Following the feast, the candles on the cake, a boisterous happy birthday song, and some dancing hinted not only to Haskell's birthday but the remnants of post-wartime celebration. Haskell's eyes filled as the joyful noise echoed his memories of old-world happy times.

Haskell held his goblet high, and his tap on its bowl brought the room to silence. He stood, a broad smile on his handsome face.

"I am pleased we are all together tonight. My only sadness is that my brother Abe is not here to celebrate with us. I am grateful that Ida and Melvin are here to share this evening with us. And most important, we are a family business. That is why there is another reason we are celebrating. Each of you will have a major decision to make."

The family fell silent. All eyes were riveted on Haskell.

"My offer is yours to accept or refuse. Please know that whatever decision you decide for yourself, I will accept without anger or remorse. This company, our company, Abraham & Haskell, has entered a time of great fortune, for which we should all be grateful. It is my intention to further share this prosperity and provide further security and comfort to those of you who will participate in my plan."

Eric called out, "What is this all about, Poppa?

"Shat, shtum [quiet, listen]. I have carefully planned an important position in the company for each of you." With a small flourish, Haskell extracted a black leather memo book from his breast pocket and reached for his eyeglasses.

"Let me begin. First, to Ida, my brother's wife: you will always own fifty percent, an equal share of the company, as Abe and I agreed. We will continue to share equally in our success." Everyone applauded as Ida acknowledged this with a smile. "Ida, this I direct to you: there will be an increased demand for women's clothes as well as men's suits, so we are making that a separate division, which you will head. And you will have a suitable salary. You like the pun—'suit-able'?" Everyone smiled at Ida.

"I want Ellen—who some of you may remember as Hannahla—to leave her job and join us as second-in-command. We will need all her skills to organize and manage every detail of running our company." He turned to his daughter. "Ellen, we will put your ambition and energy to good use." Again, more applause. Hannahla-Ellen acknowledged the announcement with her own bright smile.

"To my youngest son, Ely." All eyes turned in Ely's direction. "Eighty years ago, in 1866, my great-grandfather Havrohm brought his son Moishe, my grandfather, to work for him at fifteen. You are fifteen but still in school, although I am going to let you get your feet wet now in some part of this new venture during the summer.

"Eric, you are going to college, where you belong. After college, we can decide."

Molly shot a look and a nod that said, "I concur." Eric gritted his teeth as disappointment flashed across his face. Molly knew Eric had always imagined himself working beside his father. College had never been part of the conversation about his future.

"And, Nephew Melvin, I plan to open a retail store, or two. I have confidence in you; I need you to manage and build a great retail chain."

Melvin blinked in puzzlement, thinking, *What do I know about the retail business?* Nonetheless, he maintained his usual reserve.

From the short side of the table, next to Ellen, came a strong and confident voice. Her boyfriend, Marvin, leaped to his feet in the manner of a showman, saying, "Allow me to announce that Ellen and I have decided to get engaged, and we're making it official right now!" The room erupted in glee and shouts of "Mazel tov!" Haskell saw tears well up in his wife's eyes.

"Quiet, everyone." The room was silent, all eyes on Haskell. "I must ask my daughter a question! Did Marvin ask you to marry him?"

"Yes, Dad, he did!"

"And tell me, my Hannahla-Hannah-Ellen, what did you say?"

"I said *yes!*"

And in a crescendo of "Mazel tovs," all present toasted and embraced.

Haskell felt the warmth and happiness in the room fill him with hope. There was nowhere else Haskell would rather be. He was now on the path to redemption.

CHAPTER 20

THE FOUNDATION WIDENS

As the Brodsky business grew, the showrooms and the production floors became cramped and inefficient. Ellen and Haskell discussed renting additional floors of their building to accommodate the business's needs.

An opportunity presented itself at 100 Fifth Avenue. The building was in transition following the owner's death, and his children wished to sell the property. Their real estate agent, Matthew, was young and inexperienced, but sharp enough to see the advantages for the Brodskys to buy the building instead of taking on additional rented floors.

"Matthew, my friend, our family would not know the first thing about running a building." Haskell added that he was a seller, not a buyer, and he was not sold on the idea of the purchase. Nevertheless, he was ready to listen.

The agent countered, "Mr. Brodsky, it's not complicated. Allow me to explain. They are asking four hundred thousand dollars for the building. We should offer three hundred thousand dollars. I believe they will negotiate somewhere in the middle. You invest ten percent of the price, and the bank will lend you the rest. And presto! You and your family own a building in Manhattan, a wonderful investment that will only increase in value!"

Haskell and Hannah-Ellen considered the ups and downs, the ins and outs. "Dad, I have five thousand dollars in the bank. You and I will be partners in the building."

After a bit more wrangling about the price, they concluded the deal at $365,000 with a mortgage from the Manufacturers Trust Company on Fourteenth Street.

Haskell and Ellen offered Matthew the job of building manager. He accepted and threw in $5,000 of the commissions he earned so he would also be a small part-owner, like Ellen. Haskell, shaking his head, thought again, *New country, new things. In America, there are always new opportunities.*

CHAPTER 21

THE RECKONING

The postwar years passed with Ida, Abe's wife, as a full partner as agreed. Haskell knew, life being what it is, the day will come when it would change. It came as predicted. Ida walked into her brother-in-law's office with a sullen look. She confided in him, "I miss my Abe very much. And I am feeling lonely." He didn't speak. His head down, he moved to his chair and pointed to the one in front of his desk and invited Ida to sit. Both were silent as he poured water from a fresh pitcher on his desk into his glass.

"I understand," he said. "Molly and I speak about your lonely times often. You should take a break and go up to the Catskills; the Grossinger's or the Concord. Treat yourself. Who knows, you might make new friends."

"Haskell, you are more than a brother; you are also my friend," she said. "If Abe were alive, I would not be in your office this very moment, nor would I have the pleasure of building a business with you. But there is something else on my mind that I must share with you. It may sound insane and not worthy of a discussion."

Haskell sat quietly holding his breath, thinking, *Life has been too smooth and too easy for all of us, and somehow it is all going to change.*

With hesitation, Ida nervously began, "I have one child, Melvin. You have three wonderful children, all of whom I love dearly."

Uh-oh, here it comes. He couldn't help but expect that one day there'd be a conversation like this.

Ida continued, "It is unfair that you already have two children working at the business, and I have only Melvin. When Eric graduates from college, I know he'll want to work here as well. I find this three-to-one unfair. We are supposed to be equal partners and it is unfair that your family earns more than our family. Their salaries cut into the profits we share of the business, and your family takes a greater share of the whole."

Haskell felt a sharp voice inside caution him, accompanied by a deep pang in his chest. *Be careful, and do not begin a family war,* he thought. His head swirled with the stories of his friends who had lost children to family quarrels, whose relatives had stopped speaking to each other for years or even lifetimes in battles over money and position in the family business.

But he was unable to contain himself. "You are correct that if Abe were alive, we would never be having this conversation because your husband would have never allowed you to collaborate with him in this company. And you know that to be true. Your talents, like those of Ellen, might never have been discovered, or used without the opportunities you have enjoyed. If Abe were alive, neither you nor Ellen would be here."

Without hesitation or taking breath, he continued, "Now listen to me, Ida. Melvin is a lazy kid, and you know it. He does not resemble you or Abe. He comes in late and goes home early. He hates his job and won't even bother to acquire any new skills. Since he got married, he goes home during lunch to get laid and brags about it. You see it. You hear it. You hate it."

He caught his breath to pick up steam. His voice was no longer calm.

"On the other hand, Ellen works overtime, with gusto. She is gung ho about the business, taking meetings with vendors, visiting customers, mastering the billing, and she has organized everything in the office. As for Ely, he is busy coordinating with designers, traveling to our production sites. And Eric, who is graduating from college at the end of this year, we don't know his plans yet. If you want to start a family war, you're making a big mistake. Melvin is lucky we put up with him and pay him the same as those who are more productive to the company. The number of children we have does not figure into the family arrangement of what is fair. What's fair is Melvin, Ellen, and Ely all have the same opportunity here and are compensated equally. I ask you, my dear sister, is that fair or is the entire situation unfair?"

Haskell's eyes bored into Ida's. "What is unfair is Melvin. He is not pulling his weight, while Ellen and Ely work, work, work. *That* is what is unfair."

He was curious to see how firm Ida was in her silence. They both knew his voice was the truth. He allowed himself to be momentarily steeped in resentment. She and Melvin were not entitled to anything more, and *he* wasn't going to give in. Try as he might, Haskell couldn't grasp the measurement whereby Ida arrived at her calculation of unfairness. From his perspective, her son should have been dismissed years ago.

There was a sense of reckoning in the air.

Haskell got up from behind his desk, walked around to Ida, and placed his hand on her shoulder, assuring her, "Ida, I care about you and Melvin. You know how I value family. I want you to be safe and happy. I also want Melvin to be happy. I foresaw this, so I have been prepared for it. I have a solution."

Ida cocked her head and narrowed her eyes as she regarded Haskell carefully. Her mind raced. *What could he be planning or thinking? Would he sell this business and retire? He's not getting any younger.*

"I will buy you out," he said in a soft voice, free of any sign of aggression.

Ida was taken aback, but not so much that she was not prepared with ideas of her own. She was ready with two points that she insisted on: that they hire an independent evaluation company to inventory and appraise the company's value to set a fair sale price, and that she be part of working out the details of a mutually agreeable payout.

For his part, as a man who thought himself the epitome of fairness and as someone still punishing himself, carrying guilt over Abe's demise, it was easy for Haskell to agree.

CHAPTER 22

A NEW VENTURE

The seventh floor of their three floors at 100 Fifth Avenue would be the epicenter of the new offices. Each of the three stories connected via a custom interior staircase.

The reconstructed production facilities occupied the two lower floors. The interior staircase was Eric's idea, as well as other contributions to the business's explosive growth. Haskell enjoyed the pride he felt for his son's acumen.

Matthew, the real estate broker for the purchase of 100 Fifth, was welcome to drop by unannounced. He and Haskell together would review with relish what items fell under Matt's purview as befitting his status as (an admittedly small) part-owner in the building. Matt's foresight to acquire the building soon proved correct. Haskell's foresight to give Matt a small partnership in the building was a plus in their investment.

Haskell was delighted with Matt's street smarts, diligence, and integrity, so it wasn't hyperbole when he greeted the young man with, "Welcome, Matthew. To what do I owe the pleasure of your visit?"

"How about lunch, boss, to celebrate my thirty-eighth birthday, and then a visit to the building next door? I found out it is going up for sale."

Haskell smiled, thinking, *There must be someone watching over me. Just in time for me to think about a new challenge.* "Tell me about the building."

"It's a question of timing and proximity: the owner wants to return to his original home in Colorado. And here's the best part: next to this building, the one for sale, are two more buildings he owns!"

After a thoughtful pause, Matt closed in for his pitch with a grin: "Eventually, we could have three more buildings in a row next to ours, starting with the one next door! So can I interest you in a new venture, Mr. Haskell Brodsky?"

"Well, it never hurts to talk." Haskell chuckled, knowing he had the vision and gumption to see the trajectory, the snowballing, of what had been a tailor shop, now a player in the clothing business, into a conglomerate encompassing New York City real estate.

CHAPTER 23

THE TURNING POINT

Ida's unhappiness at her perceived unfairness of how the business provided for her and her son had Haskell hard at work on the buyout they agreed to. He was on the verge of engaging a professional evaluation company, while Ida was busy with other ideas for how they should proceed.

Haskell began the day, reflecting as he shaved, *I always do what I have to do, no matter the problem. The children, Ida and Melvin, and at work. My only weakness is firing anyone.*

He'd take the proverbial bull by the horns and vanquish it! In his running silent commentary that morning, he found himself, as a man, living up to his obligations, a quality handed down by his diligent and long-suffering ancestors. He was a good son, grandson, husband, father, and businessman. He viewed himself with a critical eye and found himself worthy.

His last conversation with Abe, that confrontation over the money he gave to the Levys, was the impetus for Abe's fateful confrontation with the "investors' club." His death was the result. It was, therefore, Haskell's responsibility to be fair with Ida.

This security was crushed by one letter he found on his desk in the den. Before he picked up the envelope addressed to "Haskell" in Ida's handwriting, he believed he was held in universal regard as scrupulous in intrafamily dealings.

As he opened the envelope, his instincts sent signals of cautiousness. He reached for his glasses and began to read.

Dear Haskell,

All future communications regarding our buyout negotiations will be through my attorney.

Ida

Haskell felt sick and tossed the letter onto his desk. It was as if the letter itself was a bolt of lightning unleashed on their family business, as if Ida had become a toxic infection. He felt he was a person of honesty, integrity, and fairness. But gone was his sense of obligation and service to his brother's widow. She would get what she deserved, what she had always been due, and not a penny less or a penny more.

"No more Mr. Nice Guy," he whispered to his reflection in the shaving mirror. *Out with the Golden Rule, in with the Silver Rule. I do to you what you do to me,* he thought. The realization energized him. He picked up the telephone to dial his attorney. He had nothing to hide, and even better, he could afford legal vindication.

This whole tangle was unnecessary, but hiring a lawyer was a signal of mistrust. It seemed to be what Ida wanted. They could have gone the easy way, in which Haskell would give his sister-in-law what she was due, but she chose the hard way, to obtain the same thing through a protracted lawsuit. His honor offended, Haskell decided to let her have her way. He justified the expensive defense he mounted as warranted to dispel Ida's unjust accusations, which were only a figment of her imagination.

Throughout the litigation, the judge's law clerk leaned on them to settle. Haskell's position was the same as ever and adhered to his agreement with Ida. Rather than engage in meaningful discussions, Ida's attorney made irrational demands.

At trial, Haskell's lawyers buried Ida's contentions with enough documents that the case never went to jury deliberations. Instead, at the conclusion of all the evidence, the judge had the parties submit directed verdict motions. Haskell's lawyer explained that when there were no questions of fact for the jury because the facts were so clear (as he put it, "The proof of the facts rise to the level of law"), only the judge can decide. And his Honor did. It was particularly satisfying that the judge's written decision, read in open court before the parties and astonished jury, declared that this was "a rare instance that no reasonable jury could decide otherwise."

The judge awarded Ida the exact offer Haskell's attorney had made pre-trial, representing a fair division as per their agreement. *Nothing more, nothing less*, Haskell thought, with satisfaction.

The judge banged his gavel then thanked the jury for their service and discharged them. Haskell rose and left the courtroom without so much as a glance in Ida's direction. *The Silver Rule.*

CHAPTER 24

KARMA

Anthony stepped off the elevator and onto Haskell's office floor one September afternoon in 1950. He took stock of the changes that time had successfully awarded the Brodskys. He admired the well-coiffed receptionist, who sat behind a walnut desk surrounded by elegantly arranged couches and chairs, end tables with lamps, and a coffee table with high-end fashion magazines. Dominating the tableaux was a staircase covered with a brightly colored custom-made Asian runner. The carpeted treads were held in place with thin, fluted brass rods.

Anthony reflected that he, too, had changed. In a confident stance with briefcase in tow, he introduced himself. Haskell's secretary, Sandra, buzzed her boss, saying, "Anthony Tracci is here to see you."

Haskell was puzzled. The name sounded familiar, but he could not place it, although he sensed a pleasant association; he was sure it would come back to him when he saw the gentleman. "Certainly! Send him in."

Sandra directed Anthony through the door on the left, and then a right turn into the office. Haskell was relieved to remember Anthony immediately, although he was now taller and well built. "Ah, Gina's son. Welcome! It's so good to see you. How's my pizza queen?"

They laughed easily. "Mama's well, thank you."

"Another prom?" Haskell teased.

"Well, not a prom . . . I am getting married."

"Congratulations! A nice Italian girl for you?"

"No, sir, a nice Jewish girl!"

Haskell swept his arm, pointing to a small sitting area with two leather armchairs and a small table between them. They sat in unison, after Anthony hesitated a moment to make sure he stood longer for etiquette's sake, a move that Haskell noted in sizing up how grown-up the young man had become. *He must be a college graduate by now. Hmm, quite an attractive young man, with the kind of strong handshake you need to succeed,* Haskell thought.

"So, tell me, where and when is the great event?"

"A Reform temple in Flatbush this coming December. I would consider it a blessing if you and Mrs. Brodsky were to join us."

"Anthony, if the Great Flood came again, we wouldn't miss it for the world! And I hope you will let us help attire you."

"I have been planning this visit for a long time. Shirley, my fiancée, said it's getting late and insisted I do it today, no more delay."

Haskell furrowed his brow into a mock query.

The young man's practiced tone was even and tinged with a palpable sense of accomplishment. "Shirley told me to kill two birds with one stone. First, I am going to pay full retail price for your best formal wear for the wedding. A tuxedo, not off the rack. I want to commission one custom-made to fit my frame since I am physically different."

Haskell was taken by Anthony's evident sense of self-respect and his mannered cadence. In response, he said, "I will have our tailor take your measurements. You remember Paul; he will show you the fabrics to pick from."

"Second, before I go to the tailor, there is something important that we must discuss," Anthony said.

Puzzled, Haskell carefully asked, "Which is what?" He was unsure where this was leading.

"My fiancée's name is Shirley Levy."

"There are so many Levys. Where are they from?"

"Her grandparents are from Lithuania. Her parents were born here in New York. She has a large family. We've met each other's families. Our cultures, our families, are more similar than different. Fortunately, neither of our families is religious. We eat, we work, we love, all the same. We plan to have both a rabbi and a priest together do the ceremony. This Reform temple will allow that. We're working through the details, like my smashing the glass to symbolize the destruction of the temple that can be said to embrace both of our religious histories."

Haskell tried to avoid wondering if he would agree to this were it his children and the tables reversed. He deliberately sounded upbeat as he pushed aside his thoughts and said, "Wonderful! I wish you health and happiness."

"But . . . back to the second purpose of why I am here . . . Please don't tell Shirley if I mangle this—tikkun olam."

Haskell was dumbstruck, both that Anthony knew the phrase and as to what it meant in this context. *Tikkun olam* is the Jewish obligation to repair the world, a bit at a time; everyone is supposed to help fix things. What could Anthony need to repair with him? Haskell could not imagine what restitution was due him.

Anthony forged ahead. "Whether I believe in God or which God, I do think if it is possible, we should try to correct the past if possible. We, Shirley and I, are two people in love. We want the best for the family and the family businesses—all of them. However, we are under a cloud."

"How so? I am no weatherman, but I am willing to help with the mission."

Anthony rose and approached Haskell's desk, put his briefcase on it, and opened the lock as if it were a sacrament. He pivoted to Haskell, caught his gaze, and when Haskell looked down at the briefcase, Anthony raised the lid. Haskell beheld wads of twenty- and fifty-dollar bills with rubber bands around them. After a silence befitting the moment, Haskell cocked his head and inquired, "You are buying tuxedos for everyone at the wedding?"

This broke the tension with a shared laugh. "You are, what's the Yiddish word for a great guy? A mensch! Trust you to defuse a tough situation with humor."

"OK, you have my attention. What's up? What is this all about?"

"Mr. Brodsky." Sandra knocked and opened the door simultaneously. Anthony closed the briefcase. "Do you or your guest want something for lunch? It's just past twelve."

Haskell looked at Anthony, who remained silent and shook his head. *No.*

In a steady voice, Haskell told her, "Sandra, not yet. I will call you when we're ready."

Haskell noticed his guest's face had turned pale and his expression grim, and he suggested they both return to sit in the alcove. He raised his eyebrows as if to say, *Go ahead.*

"I am not going to beat around the bush," Anthony said. "Do you know the Jewish investment bankers your brother Abe was involved with? They're Shirley's cousins. Thank God Shirley's branch of the family never had personal or business connections with them until Shirley and I decided to marry."

Haskell sat motionless as he tried to digest this while pushing the traumatic memory of his brother's death from his mind.

Curiosity overtook him, and he asked, "How did all this even come up?"

"When both families were all together, my mother spoke warmly of another Jewish family she knew, your son Eric, and your nephew, Melvin, emphasizing your generosity to me. She mentioned your company's name in passing. And that's when my cousin Sal looked at his Uncle Mario. His uncle from the other side of the family. They exchanged troubled looks, which the women noticed and badgered the story out of them. How Abe lost his temper, which made Morris Levy lose his, how he roughed up your brother, who fled and fell and had a heart attack, which, of course, no one intended. My mom, who's incredibly old world when it comes to superstitions, insisted that this be cleared up or it will be bad luck, even a curse on our family. Personally, Shirley and I are horrified and ashamed."

Anthony took in a long breath, and said steadily, "So as a result, last week, we had a family conclave on the Levy-banker side of the family to estimate as restitution how much profit the five thousand dollars Abe invested had been leveraged to produce. It proved an excellent investment, yielding four times the amount, about twenty thousand dollars. Along with the original five thousand dollars, it's all here, twenty-five thousand dollars, in this briefcase for you to give to your sister-in-law or to keep as restitution for the business since that's where the money came from."

Anthony shifted nervously. "This is the tikkun olam, the reparations for that sin, although nothing could bring your brother back. It is fitting that all this came to light because my mother recounted your thoughtfulness to me the day I went to get my first suit. As we approach a season of new beginnings, we must move beyond our mistakes. We want a future without the weight of this tragedy."

Haskell did not want to listen. He struggled to set aside the distractions like the telephone's flashing red light, which he ignored, and all the other things he was trying to remember that he was supposed to be doing right now. He needed to exclusively focus on the swirl of the present, as the present warped into the past, which bled into the future. Before he could think through what hinged on his decision, he gave the briefcase another glance and instinctively shook his head. He searched his conscience for clarity to this complex equation laden with conflicts, ethical and otherwise. A crime had been committed against his brother, and the entire Brodsky family was the victim. Since the money came from the business, it was due back to it. The Levys understood this tension and left it to him to work it out. This rendering was being laid at his feet, not at Ida's, a fact that was not at all lost on him.

Judgments did not completely form before other, newer, thoughts crowded them out. On the one hand, while this gesture was framed as reparations or restitution, was it, in effect, a bribe? On the other hand, if Abe died of a heart attack, how complicit were the Levys, really? They didn't mean to kill him. Ida didn't need the money, nor did their business. Were there tax implications? The entire endeavor was unfamiliar territory, which he realized was fraught with consequences he knew he could not fully foresee.

His inner voice reminded and reassured him that he could be counted on to do what needed to be done with grace and respect. He felt fortunate that he could manage a mantle of magnanimity. "No, I cannot accept this money," he said. "The business wanted no part of this matter from the beginning. I can speak for the family when I say, with all due respect, that you cannot put a price on life."

Haskell paused, feeling the stillness in the room. "I am afraid this might be misunderstood as blood money. Accepting it dishonors my brother and our family. Unfortunately, my brother made many mistakes, and his final blunder was his greatest and a series of errors that cost him everything, cost him his life."

Anthony fought to take a breath, paralyzed by the thought that he had failed both his family and the Brodskys as he waited for Haskell to continue.

"I am sorry, I cannot allow myself to consent to your request," Haskell said. "I regret I cannot accept a single cent. Our forgiveness does not in any way include monetary repayments. On behalf of my own family, my wife, and children, to the extent you believe absolution is up to us, you are all forgiven for your errors. Tell your wonderful mother, whom I admire and care about, that I believe your side of the Tracci family had no guilt in the incident leading to the tragedy we all lived through. And I hold no bad feelings for any other side of the Tracci family, either. We wish you all health and happiness."

Anthony's eyes swelled with tears. As he and Haskell stood, he grasped both of Haskell's hands in his. "Mr. Brodsky, you are truly a mensch! I hope I learn from your example, that I am always the bigger man in any situation I find myself. I will always be in debt to you for showing me what a real mitzvah [blessing] is."

Haskell smiled approvingly. "I am impressed with your Yiddish."

Anthony relaxed as he shared his efforts to learn a smattering of Yiddish, which had delighted Shirley. It had become a point of pride for him.

"I have discovered how expressive Yiddish words can be, and how Shirley and I can blend our two-family cultures. Italians and Jews, cousin clans, now kissing cousins, yes? It's about bringing families together. You have a Yiddish word for your people, for compatriots from the old country. A great word: "landsman.""

Italians and Jews, they are landsman cousins. We are more alike than not, I have discovered."

This is America now, Haskell thought. *But I can only envision my two unwed children marrying fellow Jews, and I am loath to explicitly approve religious intermarriage.* He lifted his right hand and let it drop noncommittally, then wobbled his head slightly in a circle as if dizzy in a humorous suggestion of disagreement. "Oh, these new American ways!"

He could discern that Anthony wanted his blessing beyond the intermarriage aspect, or even beyond burying the hatchet about his brother.

"Mr. Brodsky, allow me to be frank. When I was a boy and came to your shop, my father had been dead a long while. We were barely acquainted, and that I was not of your religion, these things did not matter. As you welcomed me, and clothed me, you were as kind and encouraging—not to mention, generous—as if I were your son, not a stranger. I was every son to you as you dressed me. I didn't want to leave, and when I did, I left idolizing you. I thought of you as the father I wanted, that I needed and deserved. Mama cried when I told her how well you treated me. She said you were a saint. I don't think you have saints in Judaism, but this is quite a distinction. When I am short on kindness, but the situation demands it, I think back to how you took me under your wing and I left feeling like a million dollars. Did you know you did that for me?"

All else fell away and Haskell didn't want to disturb this poignant moment by even breathing. He blocked out the sounds of traffic and the draft from the open window. Then he inhaled sharply and spoke again, "Thank you for your kind words. Please forgive me, the answer is no. I cannot accept this money."

Anthony paused to consider and reimagine the possibilities. "Please, Mr. Brodsky, for my mother's sake and her superstitions, I must end all controversy within and outside the families touching on this matter. True, we cannot undo the past. But we can soften it. I will meet your objections. I am authorized to present you with this money with the charge that, as penitence for our families, it goes to a charity of your choice, or one you think Abe would have approved of. It doesn't have to be an actual charity; perhaps there's a needy family who attends your synagogue who could use some help. You helped me when I needed it. Let this help someone else."

Against his best intentions, Haskell was persuaded. "This I can do."

The matter settled, Haskell shifted away from the topic to ask Anthony, "Where are you working now?"

"I am an assistant to the director of sales at a printing company in lower Manhattan. It's decent work. I like working hard, I enjoy being busy. The busier I am, the happier I am."

Haskell found he felt a true affection for this young man. "How would you like to join our firm as assistant director of sales—in training?"

A look of studied reflection came over Anthony. He squinted as he scrutinized Haskell's expression. Then he said simply, "I would like very much to come and work with you."

They shook hands, shared a laugh, and pulled each other close, embracing. Haskell said casually, as if this happened all the time, "Today I will take the money to our rabbi and in memory of Abraham Brodsky, give it to the rabbi's discretionary fund, which he uses to disperse gelt [money] to our poor and infirm. Sad to say there are many. For your part, assure your mother that under Jewish law, by this act of charity and tikkun olam, any cloud over this marriage or your families is lifted, and heaven itself will forbid any bad luck in the marriage of Shirley and Anthony Tracci." Haskell smiled. "Furthermore, my pizza queen will live to see your marriage blessed with children and grandchildren."

At this, Anthony took his leave with a kiss to Haskell's cheek, his hand cupping his shoulder. "See you in shul!" he said.

"Call me about your start date," Haskell said. "We run a tight ship. I will see you on board."

CHAPTER 25

IT ISN'T EASY BEING THE BOSS

Advancing age has its consequences. For Mr. Brodsky, it meant too much noise, less patience with people, and diminishing memory. He could be more forgiving of his own shortcomings because other people were there to pick up the slack, but when they didn't or didn't do their job effectively, he was not as patient. For example, writing well-written business letters was not in Haskell's skill set. Instead, as he conducted his business through telephone conversations and face-to-face meetings, he got what he needed or wanted by deftly wielding a conversational tone and the confident, informed casualness he'd first mastered in his father's clothing and tailor shop and perfected with years of negotiating with his clients.

It was the end of the week and there were letters he had intended to send, but now it was already Friday, and they weren't ready. As he read over the letters prepared by Sylvia, his secretary, he was struck that her writing was as unimpressive as if he'd written them himself—which he hadn't. Haskell had dictated them, but Sylvia was expected to polish them. Yet her work was routinely underwhelming. She had been with him long enough and was paid adequately. He expected her to do better by now.

Haskell called to his daughter in the adjacent office, "Hannahla, please come into my office."

Ellen walked briskly into her father's space, and with an arched edge to her voice, said, "Dad, I am too old for this. I thought we agreed to only call me 'Ellen'—Mom does!"

Everyone's giving me tsuris [misery]. First Sylvia, now Hannahla, the old man reflected. *I never stopped calling her Hannahla in my head, and I'm good about calling her Ellen to her face. What's with her tone of voice? Is something wrong with me, or is it her? Am I getting too old, too tired, to pay attention? Am I expected to always understand my children when I can hardly understand myself?*

He fought back his impatience and said evenly, "I am sorry, dear; you know I hardly ever do that anymore. Please have a seat, Ellen. I have a problem I want you to help with."

Ellen broke into a small smile at this indication of progress. "What is it? I'm glad to help if I can."

Haskell rubbed his thumb in circles on his forehead to ease the headache that accompanied his thoughts. "Sylvia is as bad a writer as I am, and I didn't learn English until late, not like Sylvia, who was born here speaking it. If I dictate a badly worded letter, I get back the same without improvements, often with spelling and typing mistakes. She's not doing what needs to be done; I need someone better. You are my office manager—I want you to fire her!"

Ellen shook her head slowly for emphasis and said, "You're the boss—you fire her."

It was true that being the boss was a role he inhabited, enjoyed, and if he said so himself, excelled in—except in this one regard. Firing someone was his most painful business task. He hated to even say it aloud, but he did: "I hate firing anyone. You are a boss now, too, so please get rid of Sylvia and find me a new secretary. Give her five months' severance."

He knew himself to be both a shrewd businessperson and an empathetic employer, proclivities traceable to his struggles in Poland related to work and food and creature comforts. He had seen suffering and was loath to be its cause, so he avoided firing people. Surely Hannahla-Ellen would see this as a good thing and help him out.

Ellen rose from her seat to draw herself up to her full height, and her voice was tight but strong as she said, "Dad, it's not my job to fire a person that you hired. When someone I brought into the company needs to be fired, then I'll fire them. You hire, you fire. That's the rule."

She became bemused. "Dad, it seems anomalous, being the person of action that you are, for you to resist doing this one task."

She doesn't see my hesitation as a good thing, Haskell thought.

Ellen eyed her father, and he felt the meaning of her stare, of her unwillingness to help, a battle between sympathy and even a touch of irritation for his uncharacteristic weakness. He was on the losing end as mutual disappointment hung in the air.

Ellen was not letting her father off the hook. "You hired her. You fire her."

She held her ground. *I must follow everybody else's rules, but this is my rule. America is the land of reinvention for everyone else; here I am not an underling anymore, I am equal, I am a partner. I make rules, too. Being a woman is not going to hold me back. Not even if my father insists.*

After a few awkward moments of silence, Ellen said with forced lightness, "Then, I'll leave you to it. Good luck."

With no way out, Haskell watched an hour tick by. He called Sylvia into his office. She went to the chair opposite him, as was her practice, and sat down with a pencil and stenographic pad poised in her hands and lap. She sensed something was wrong and returned his gaze with what he could see was genuine concern. He thought to begin slowly by saying, "Sylvia, there are a few errors in these letters. Please correct them."

Suddenly, she got right up. "Yes, sir, Mr. Brodsky!" she said and immediately gathered the letters. She was gone before he could continue his planned remarks.

An hour later the retyped letters were on his desk without any errors or basis on which he could complain. He sighed. "Thank you, Sylvia. That was fast."

She said in a soft voice, "I know you like to leave early on Friday. Good night, Mr. Brodsky, Shabbat Shalom [good Sabbath]. Have a great weekend."

"You, too," he managed to mumble while stewing in his cowardice, left to ponder whether he had been outmaneuvered. Something about her demeanor made him suspect she had known the end was coming.

After the weekend, when the situation with his daughter seemed to smooth out, Haskell went to Ellen's office. "It would be nice if you, Eric, and I had lunch today; my treat."

"Dad, it's always your treat!"

He liked a noon lunchtime, and so Haskell, his daughter, and his son sat at their regular table in Hammer's restaurant. They were greeted with a warm and genuine welcome.

Selma, the manager, sent over a metal tray filled with an assortment of house appetizers. Eric and Hannahla-Ellen dug in. Haskell was pleased to see his children blessed with hearty appetites.

"So how do you like working for us this summer?" he asked Eric.

"I am really enjoying it, Dad, but I could use a raise."

Haskell chuckled. Eric was funny, like he was himself at the beginning of his career, a chip off the old block.

"Ah ha! That's the Brodsky spirit I know! Next year!" They all laughed.

"Dad, can I have a beer?"

"Don't ask me, Eric, until you are twenty-one, which you will be shortly. Then you won't have to ask me."

Hannahla-Ellen frowned and said, "As your sister and the office manager, you should never, never drink during work hours, no exceptions. I don't care who else does or who asks you to join them. And, for your information, they do not serve beer here, thank goodness."

Haskell thought, *It's not just that he's my son. Eric's handsome, smart, hardworking, the whole package.*

"You know something, young man," he said, "I was thinking, maybe someday if you decide to join the company, you may become the boss."

Ellen interjected, "What am I? Chopped liver?"

"Sounds great," Eric said. He often mused about how fortunate he was to have this family heritage, a family business. It carried a powerful sense of duty. Even before coming to America, the business was built by his grandfather Solomon, Solomon's father, Moishe, and Moishe's father, Havrohm. They, and his father, Haskell, had all earned their success. Eric mused that he would merely inherit. He wondered if he would one day be able to say that he himself had earned his success. He wanted the esteem awarded those who accomplished things themselves; he did not want to be a man whose success would be chalked up to mere luck or sneered at as a member of the "lucky sperm club."

Eric decided to concentrate on building a reservoir of skills, even as he understood he was too young to know what skills needed to be encompassed. Yes, his family liked to have a good time, but he was able to see that, on the verge of turning twenty-one, the kidding around of childhood was over.

"Well, if you want to be a boss, you can begin today."

"What do I have to do?" the young man asked with a chuckle.

"Today, when we return to the office, I want you to fire Sylvia."

"Dad!" Ellen scowled. Haskell gave her a look and said, "I am not kidding."

Eric knew enough to keep quiet after that, as he raised an eyebrow in his sister's direction.

"Dad, think about this," Ellen said. "How would Sylvia feel to be fired by a twenty-one-year-old? She would feel devalued, even angry. That is not like you."

The next Friday afternoon, Haskell brought Sylvia into his office to settle the matter. Kindly, he told her that things were no longer working out between them, thanked her for her years of service to him and the business, and handed her a check he had prewritten for six months' severance (instead of five, like he had instructed Hannahla to give her).

Rarely was Haskell surprised, but Sylvia surprised him. "I am so very grateful for the five-year relationship we had," she said. "I was proud to be part of Abraham & Haskell. I liked being part of the staff, but I feel like you outgrew me along the way, and I'm sorry. I hope you find the right person soon. You are a good and decent man."

The part that surprised him was her recognition of the underlying truth: as business grew, she didn't. He was taken with her maturity. He was sorry it had come to this, but *business was business,* he thought.

Eric must have seen what happened because after Sylvia left, he came in and stood over Haskell with a protective look. "Dad, I could have fired Sylvia for you. I would have." He kissed his father and said, "I love you, Dad."

Even though Haskell felt uncomfortable about firing Sylvia, he was delighted with Eric. To kvell was one of life's rewards, but he did not want Eric to mistake the tears now stinging his eyes for doddering, so he composed himself and said with a false casualness, "Go home, now. You worked hard this week. Shabbat Shalom!"

CHAPTER 26

ERIC'S TURN

Eric graduated from City College of New York in the class of 1950. He was the first of his family to earn a college degree. This pride, the rite of passage when a family lives to celebrate their first college graduate, was infused with the sense of respect for their immigrant ancestors who undertook the passage from the old world to the new. During the family celebration, Eric made a point to acknowledge the challenging work and sacrifices of those who paved the way. He also acknowledged his parents and the family legacy that enlivened their commitment to hard work, honesty, and their family target of success. Achieving a degree was the first step.

A few months before graduating, Haskell formally extended an invitation for Eric to join the family business. "But before you answer," Poppa advised, "I believe it will be an important experience in your life to work elsewhere first. You'll want to know that you can stand on your own two feet without me there to protect you. Go where it's competitive, where you are not given the benefit of the doubt or adored, where you will be under pressure to succeed. Join a firm where you will be held to the highest standards."

Eric shared his father's perspective. The same thoughts had been running through his head for months. In college he'd befriended several fellow students who had nothing to fall back on, no family business, sometimes no family at all. Still, they were fully confident they would find their own way to success. He wondered if he would be as self-assured without the family business backstop and began to suspect that moving from college to work with his father was not what he wanted. This was indeed the time to strike out on his own.

Haskell said, "If you have the skills to sell a suit and coat, you can sell a skyscraper! It's in your genes!"

Eric soon landed a position in a prominent architectural firm in Manhattan. He set out to succeed. He never failed to appear impeccably attired, as befitting a young man who came from a clothing family. He deployed the same work ethic—the rectitude and productivity he had acquired at Abraham & Haskell. A combination of style and substance brought him a rapid promotion as assistant to the junior partner, and a place at the table where important corporate opportunities were considered. On occasion, he was asked to weigh in on more important matters by the firm's principals. Noticing his tenor and grasp of information, a promotion to the firm's "pitch team" for new bids and projects followed.

The position appealed to both his creative and business side. It provided an education in the new profitable sector of architecture, where firms designed, built, and managed buildings, and his responsibilities brought him into contact with clients, partners, suppliers, all manner of movers and shakers in his sprawling city. Through them, he discovered his love of variety: people, projects, neighborhoods, and especially anything international. After spending his entire life in New York City, he was bit by wanderlust. Without a family of his own or other commitments to hold him back, Eric promoted himself as eager and able to make business excursions. This stood him in good stead.

After accompanying executives to make project pitches in Canada and Mexico, he earned the opportunity to be posted to

Taiwan, where he was responsible for overseeing an entire project, the design and construction of a major library. He applied himself to being meticulous at every step, including respecting local customs. All these natural skills brought the project to a successful conclusion within budget and on time. In a letter back to the firm that was shared with him, the Asian client team praised Eric's skills, diligence, and competence.

In the world of tailoring and clothing sales, one unceasingly used the powers of observation of changes and trends. So it was that Eric fancied himself the keen observer of any hallmarks of success, the better to adapt them to his own use. Early in his career, Eric realized that being brought up to recognize patterns was a skill portable to other businesses and equally valuable. In place of his father's swatches and samples, Eric had architects' tools of the trade: models, blueprints, materials, tools, labor, and a polished finish.

Eric continued his transformation to adulthood by moving out of his parents' apartment to a small apartment on the Lower East Side with roommates in a borderline neighborhood known for drunks and fleabag hotels. His college friends Jonathan and Emily shared a bedroom, and he had the other. With a salary of eighty-five dollars a week, a monthly rent of twenty-eight dollars was a comfortable stretch.

He joined his family every Friday evening for a home-cooked Shabbat dinner, during which they swapped stories of their week.

Now that college and the issue of work were settled, inevitably the elephant in the room had to come up. When they were alone in the den, Haskell asked, "Tell me, my son, how are things with you? Do you have a girlfriend?"

"I have two girlfriends, Poppa. But I am so busy at work, it's difficult."

"Is it too hard to do the job and have a girlfriend?"

"No, I meant that it's stressful to date two girlfriends at the same time. The job I love. That makes it easy; I enjoy going to work every day."

Haskell listened carefully. "It pleases me to hear you enjoy your job. Life is so much better if you look forward each day to going to your office or your factory or visiting a customer. Success comes when you love your work; failure is the dread you experience going to work. The other half to a successful life is to find and keep the love of a good woman, like your mother. It's reassuring to know that you are well on your way in pursuit of both love of work and love of a good woman."

This was Haskell's life and philosophy: work and love. His were the actions of a businessman; it coursed in his blood and served him well. Like many immigrants, the Brodsky family enjoyed bonds of gratitude and dedication to one's career and family. *Eric is a chip off the old block*, he thought. "Come, Momma will be upset if we miss her babka and the mandel bread [almond cake] she made special for you."

Eric leaned over and kissed his father. "Love you, Dad."

"Love you back, my boy," Haskell said, feeling every cell in his body smile.

CHAPTER 27

THE THIEF

Haskell's new secretary, Sandra, called on the office intercom, "Bernie from the zipper company is here to see you. He doesn't have an appointment."

Jeez, Haskell thought, a bit stunned, *I haven't seen Bernie in . . . over eight years, not since my Hannah's wedding. I hope he isn't retiring.*

"Send him in. He's an old friend."

Bernie came into Haskell's office; he had a slight stoop and used a cane. *Ever the dandy, he is always put together*, Haskell noted. The elder gentleman gazed around. A smile tickled his lips, and his eyes shone in wonderment.

"Nice office, Haskell, my friend. We have come a long way, nu [true]. Where shall I sit?"

Haskell motioned to the sofa and called out to Sandra through the ajar door, "Please bring in two bottles of seltzer water. Thank you."

"Right away, Haskell."

Bernie raised an eyebrow and asked, "Your secretary calls you 'Haskell'?"

"You can't fight progress. It's a new world. Here in America, everything and everyone is more casual."

Bernie continued to survey the furnishings, including the paintings on the wall and family photographs. Fashion magazines neatly on the coffee table. "You are so right. It is a new world."

"You either adjust, or go down the tubes," Haskell noted philosophically. He couldn't contain his curiosity, reaching over and touching his friend on the knee. "OK, Bernie, so what's up with you? Your family is good, thank God. To what do I owe the pleasure of this visit?"

Sandra brought in the water, a straw in each glass, and two napkins, then shut the door as she left.

Bernie began, "It's good that we are alone. I would have spoken to Hannah, I mean, Ellen, about this issue, but it is too close to her life. Too close to all our lives."

Haskell felt his stomach pitch. "Hannah can deal with anything. She is a force of nature."

"No, my friend, this is not for Hannah, this is for you." The heaviness in Bernie's voice was suffocating.

"So, tell me already!"

"Your son-in-law, Marvin," he paused dramatically, "is a fucking son of a bitch crook!"

Automatically, Haskell rose from his seat. "You and I are friends; we have been doing business for more than thirty years, and you come here with lies like that! How dare you? You have a hell of a nerve." He felt disemboweled, knowing something was very wrong in spite of his defense of his son-in-law.

Bernie pushed ahead. "We have been your supplier for buttons and zippers and linings for thirty years. We have had our differences, mostly in terms of price and rarely about delivery. Agreed?"

"So, Marvin is busting your balls about delivery?"

"Haskell, you are not aware that we have not done business with you for more than a year. Our competitor is giving Marvin a five percent payoff, a bribe you could call it. We would not meet his demand for the kickback because you know we never do that for anyone. It's dishonest and we could go to jail."

Haskell was at a loss for words. He thought his head would pop off and roll into a corner. Dizziness crushed him; he felt nauseous, and it was a miracle that he found his voice. "How do you know that is true?"

"First, Marvin must be the stupidest putz alive. Your brainless son-in-law asked my Arnold for a confidential five percent kickback. As if I would stab you in the back, ruin a friendship of decades! We went to Marvin and Hannah's wedding, for Chrissake."

Haskell's shock did not, for a single moment, formulate into the question: Why didn't I see this before? Other thoughts vied for his attention: *the Porsche, the trip to Chicago. Oy vey, why could I not see it? I could think of many such things, now all suspicious.*

Haskell shifted to thoughts of his friend's business. "How much business of ours have you lost?"

"Since Marvin took our zipper contract elsewhere, for the past year or so, we're out about $325,000."

Haskell calculated the kickback: $16,250, and that was only from his zipper and button vendor. There were other vendors to consider, too.

Bernie felt compelled to explain, "I wanted to go to Hannah, uh, to Ellen, but my son convinced me that only you should know about it. We talked it over and decided that only you can figure out how to solve it."

"Your son was right; you were both right. Thank you, Bernie; thank you for your loyalty. I will let you know what happens." Haskell felt as if he had imploded and sank into his chair in silence.

His face etched with pity, Bernie leaned over to shake Haskell's hand and said solemnly, "Good-bye. I'll see myself out. You sit there. It's a lot to digest."

Haskell's world dissolved. He sat, feeling disconnected and disoriented by this new reality. The betrayal penetrated him, and he began bleeding rage. The sense of déjà vu revolted him as the ghost of his brother Abe taking $5,000 haunted him. He couldn't believe he had been fooled again. He bent and dropped his head into his palms.

CHAPTER 28

A few days later, Haskell sat quietly at his desk. *Here I am, Hannahla's father, the owner of the company, so smart, so clever.* He knew everything now. Shaking, heart thumping, he spoke to the empty chair: "How could I have been so stupid. There were clues. I let them pass." The chair did not answer; it stood in place silently. He reached for his phone. "Sandra, please have both Ellen and Marvin in my office at the top of the hour, at four o'clock. I have some good news to share with them. And, Sandra, no calls, no interruptions under any conditions." To himself he whispered, "You thought you were smart, a genius. You love your daughter too much, too hard. You failed to see the signals. You're a putz."

"Will do, boss," Sandra responded in her can-do voice.

He ran through his script, setting out the props in plain sight: a folder teeming with papers, a recording device, the photography store envelope, another envelope torn open, and a small black box.

Haskell weighed which offense was greater: that bastard cheating on his daughter or cheating the family business. He wanted this meeting to encompass both; this would be the first and last blow-out. As the hour approached, he pondered, *What does it mean, or say about me, that I regard embezzlement as stealing from my children?*

Ellen came in first, a minute early. "Hey, Dad, what's up? I was in the showroom with the buyers from Los Angeles. They're reviewing our fall collection."

"I know, so I sent in Anthony. He will take it from there. We have some significant news that you are an essential part of, and it will require the rest of the afternoon. Please, have a seat in the armchair."

Marvin came in hesitantly. Haskell greeted him with a forced smile, telling himself that this was the last time he would do so. "Come, have a seat in the other armchair."

Haskell stood in front of his desk, leaning back a bit, which was unusual. His arms coiled around him. He watched Marvin fidget like a snake charmer watches his cobra, and thought, *I am a snake to this lizard; I will devour him.*

"Well," Haskell said, clasping his hands together, "we are gathered here for some interesting news that will change all our lives."

"I can't wait!" Ellen said enthusiastically.

"First, Marvin, you weren't around for the visit from my old friend Bernie Tuchman, from the button, zipper, and lining company," Haskell said. "You know, the one we've done business with for decades, since you were in diapers. The man is a prince; he was the first to extend a line of credit to us, when no one else would."

Haskell watched Marvin's complexion first flash red, then drain of blood to deathly white. *This moron better not get sick on my carpet,* he thought. Ellen watched her father stare at her husband with a look of hate and disgust. The pleasant expression on her face vanished.

"Bernie told me of your trying to draw him into a criminal scheme for kickbacks, and so I investigated several things, including your business jaunts to Chicago and elsewhere, the times you went without my daughter. You are lucky that I am going to let you crawl away instead of calling the police."

Marvin's eyes reddened as he plucked at his lip nervously.

Oh shit, is he going to vomit or cry? What a pathetic, useless asshole, Haskell thought.

Ellen leaped to her feet, radiating an overwhelming sense of power, more than her husband ever had. She stood before her father, furious, her face in his face. "How dare you! How dare you stage this! How dare you accuse Marvin!" Her voice plowed into her father.

Haskell looked straight into his daughter's eyes. He was silent. Turning to Marvin, away from where Ellen stood, he said, "Was I not clear? You cheat on my daughter, you son of a bitch."

Swiveling to the sniveling Marvin, Haskell uncoiled an arm to gesture to the items arrayed on his desk, unrelenting. "You are a traitor to our company and to your family. I have the damned proof here, you moron! So now, in front of my daughter, your wife, admit what I say is true, or we can review piece by piece the ugly evidence of your disgusting secret life."

Marvin started to stutter stupid explanations: "Bernie's prices were high; their deliveries were always late! Their company also had high minimums." His weak protestations were ignored.

Ellen's gaze followed her husband's eyes to the items on her father's desk. With the realization that they contained the ruination of her marriage, she sank back into her chair, choking, the wind knocked out of her. In the next moment, she got up to snatch them, but Haskell was prepared and swept them aside, out of her reach.

"Ellen, let's see if your philandering asshole husband has the balls to confess what happened in Chicago at the last show. What has been his practice on business trips? Then take my advice, go to your doctor, and make sure you don't have gonorrhea or some other disease from this lowlife."

At this, Ellen gasped and started sobbing.

Marvin gathered up his puny attempt at indignation. "I am paid less than I merit."

Haskell launched into him with sarcasm. "Let's ask the rabbis, consult the Talmud: What does a thief merit? What does a coward merit? Do you need more money; you think you deserve more money? Do you know what a mensch does? He stands up like a man and makes his argument. You persuade people because you're right. You don't steal; you don't betray. You're rotten through and through. Get your stinking existence out of my sight, out of this office, and out of my daughter's life. You know me well enough to know I am hiring New York's best divorce attorney. At the slightest provocation, I will have you raked over the coals, and into prison. So be smart for once in your miserable life, get the fuck out and stay out! Make sure we never hear from you again, or you will live to regret it. And, you idiot, this is the best deal you ever got."

Ellen's tears subsided long enough for her to look at Marvin as if she had never seen her husband before. Her lips curled in disgust. "Marvin, I don't even know who you are." She turned to confront her father. "How long have you known these things, Dad?"

"Not for long. I am outraged that you've been played for a fool. But I say, as your father, that this piece of shit is done here, and if he gives me or you any shit, I will press charges for embezzlement and whatever else his dishonest ass warrants."

"Dad, what choice do I have in the matter?"

"There's no choice to have a thief continue in the business, and why would you choose to disgrace yourself by staying married to a cheat?"

He turned to Marvin, who was squirming in his chair, impatient to cut the process short. "Let me tell you something, Mr. Big Shot. I have always treated you like a son: I trusted you and I loved you. You had me fooled, too, for a while. I let you manage an important part of our business, gave you opportunities that would have led to family partnership. Instead, to your shame, you stabbed us in the back. Don't think I haven't the proof that you have taken bribes from other suppliers."

Haskell bore down on Marvin. "How could you be so disloyal to the business, and your wife, to the entire family? H. Jackson Brown Jr. said that character is what you are when no one is looking. And when no one is looking, you are a cheat—in your business and in your family. In your case, I don't know if either one alone is forgivable, but together they spell doom. You are out of our future, our lives, and hopefully out of the life of my daughter."

Haskell brought his face close enough so Marvin could feel the heat of his breath. "You are fired! You are a disgusting piece of shit," he shouted, his teeth gritting, his face deathly pale.

He stood back up to take in the shrunken measure of his son-in-law, a man exposed for what he was. The moment of exile had come, and Haskell commanded, "For daring to do this to our family, our business, and to my daughter: Get out. You can take your coat and nothing else. Whatever's yours, we will put it in a box and send it to you. You are dead to us! Tomorrow, we sit shiva."

Marvin sat paralyzed with terror, glued to the armchair. Haskell yanked him to his feet, although that had not been part of the plan. He cast his detested son-in-law from his office, as if from Eden, stripped naked of all but his well-deserved humiliation.

Marvin stumbled out of the office. A look of painful regret showed through the tears on Ellen's face. She stood deflated, frozen, and once again slumped silently in her chair.

Haskell felt his soaking shirt against his back. Despite his racing heart and heavy perspiration, he walked to the cabinet behind his desk and got the open bottle of whiskey. He did not bother to pour it into a glass; instead, he closed his eyes in a momentary prayer, raised the whiskey to his lips, drank deeply, swilled the drink around his mouth, and swallowed. *Not enough*, he thought, and followed it with another long swig. He collapsed heavily into the chair next to his daughter.

He remembered Ellen refusing to fire his former secretary. She had taunted him, "You hire, you fire." Well, he had hired Marvin, and now he had fired him. He was convinced Ellen needed to do the same to her husband. He remembered his Silver Rule: "Do unto others as they do unto you."

Dazed, Ellen murmured to Haskell, "You just destroyed my world."

"Marvin did, Ellen my dearest, not me. He did it all by himself."

She looked like a little girl. Ellen raised her palms, shook her head, and just asked, "Why?"

"Nothing is as it appears to be, nor is it otherwise," her father replied.

They let that hang in the air for what seemed an endless moment.

"What was the good news?" she asked.

"The truth is the good news."

She looked at him in disbelief.

Just then the red light blinked on Haskell's phone, and a few seconds later Sandra tapped on his door. She dipped her head in and said, "Mr. Brodsky, your grandson Benjamin is on the line."

Haskell shook his head. *No.* He could not talk to Ellen's son in that moment.

"His babysitter put him on the phone to ask if his mother is with you and when she will be home."

"Tell him yes and soon. And please, close the door. I said not to disturb us for any reason."

Turning to his daughter, he murmured her childhood name, his mother's name, "Hannahla, Hannahla."

He waited a few more beats. "Your husband is without honor, unfit for you. Unfit for the family business. He is a small man, unworthy of you. You deserve better than a liar and a fool. How many ways did he put you in harm's way: personal, social, physical, financial, even possibly criminal? I am here to tell you, you deserve more!" She nodded as she sobbed.

His voice had softened until it was barely audible, but his words were still harsh. "Marvin was stupid to risk such disgrace, stupid to think that he would get away with it. Where's his soul, his values, his promises to you? Nowhere! He loves only himself; he values only material things. His behavior with other women has been wanton and reckless. He either thought that you were too stupid to see what was going on, or that you would endure his lies, insults, and injuries. Greed and materialism were his only concerns, not you and not Benjamin. My investigation so far has uncovered over a hundred thousand dollars in kickbacks and cheating on his expense reports. And I will spare you the details of his involvement with other women. It is all intolerable."

He knew what was coming, knew his daughter's world was disintegrating, so he did not expect her to be composed. Ellen heaved with waves of wailing that surely Sandra could hear.

As he had imagined this would unfold, to shore her up, he now unfurled as much fatherly advice as he could channel, from time immemorial. "This is about is your marriage, yes, and it is about our business. These are not mistakes easily overlooked; they are unforgivably crushing blows to our hearts."

He reached for the freshly pressed handkerchief that was always in his pocket. "Hannahla, dry your eyes. True, sometimes affairs are forgiven because people in marriages make mistakes. From my experience in life, the man is usually at fault. But leaving aside Marvin's adultery—that is, his lack of impulse control—what's his excuse for stealing from the company, which is stealing from all of us, including you and even his son? Stealing takes strategy, tactics, and repeated sneaky efforts, a pattern of willful deceit over time. There are always many victims."

He placed his hands on Ellen's shoulders as if to bestow the children's blessing. With as much compassion as he could muster, Haskell said to his beloved daughter, "You are still a young and beautiful woman. There are so many men who are good and kind and would give you the love you want and need. Men who will not disrespect you."

Ellen looked up to meet her father's gaze. "In time you will find consolation," he said. "There are men and women who lose their partners from illness or an accident. They mourn and go on. Look at your Aunt Ida. Didn't she find a new life for herself with a nice widower? She loves him more than she loved my brother."

He stood back a little and ventured a smile as a peace offering. He extended his hand, to help her up in a gallant gesture she found a little silly, and she stifled her sniffles. "Remember yourself. Remember who you are, what you are worthy of, and this advice from my own father: 'Not all things that are true in your life are also sad.' Remember Benjamin," he told her as he saw her out.

As soon as he sat back down at his desk, his head pounded and he said a silent prayer, "Please, let my daughter forgive me; don't let my grandson hate me." He picked up the telephone and cleared his throat. "Sandra, bring me two aspirin."

"Yes, sir!" Her positive tone gave him hope. *I can do this*, he thought. *I did what had to be done, and it is done, thank God.*

CHAPTER 29

NOTHING IS AS IT APPEARS TO BE

Haskell calmed down, talking to the empty chair, thinking about Abe and how much he missed his brother. He resisted having another whiskey. Sandra peeked in and snapped him out of his deep thoughts.

"Your son Eric is coming to your home for dinner tonight. Mrs. Brodsky telephoned and asked me to remind you." The Marvin and Ellen hurricane over, Sandra stayed put until she knew he was managing.

"Thanks, Sandra. It will be a relief to be with Eric."

"It's Shabbat; I'm sure everyone is waiting for you at home. Let's both leave now."

The aroma of Molly's cooking surrounded Haskell, working its magic the moment he stepped off the elevator and consciously shifted from office mode to his husband manner, from workweek to Friday evening Shabbat. In the kitchen, Molly turned from the stove in her apron and a sweetheart's smile graced her crinkled face. Swiftly, he crossed the room to give her an embrace to please her and himself. He needed her warmth, her special hug.

Before anything else could happen, Eric burst through the door. "I'm home," he called out, "and exactly on time! It's six! This place smells delicious! What's on the menu, Momma?"

"Everything you like," she replied, unable to suppress a grin of maternal pride.

"Hey, Poppa! How was your week? Not too tiring, I hope. I know you say it's hard being the boss." He laughed, this lanky, younger image of Haskell, with his tousled hair.

What care does he have? Youth is wasted on the young, Haskell thought half-seriously, *but if so, it should be wasted on one as glorious as this boy.*

Haskell motioned Eric to follow him into the living room over to the liquor hutch. The day had already wrought a momentous change, and he could use a drink to decide how to broach the equally momentous consequences. But first he wanted to stop time, to simply savor basking in Eric's presence, in the vitality of his own flesh and blood. He fixated on his son, thinking that somehow, Eric combined an easy carriage of success with a lack of pretension. He reminded himself that his grandfather Solomon had said to him, "Timing is everything" in terms of approaching a sale. Now was the time to sell Eric on joining the company. A moment of regret flashed through his mind. He feared he had waited too long to have his son back in the family business.

At the hutch, Eric—or, as Haskell often thought of him, *Eric the college graduate*—poured them each a Scotch, neat, in the clear tumblers. They clinked glasses and said in unison, "L'chaim [To life]!"

Haskell was glad his son was of age to enjoy sharing a drink with him. It was time to replace Marvin with Eric.

"So, how is my architect? Making a living?" Poppa began.

"I'm just a beginner. I'm doing fine. I like the situation, the people, the atmosphere."

"I'm happy if you're happy," Poppa replied.

"I am happy, but not fulfilled. It is a good place to get my bearings."

Haskell hesitated. "How long does that take?"

"What take?"

"How long does it take to get your bearings?"

"I don't know, several years, I guess. I am learning a lot."

"Is it the right place for you?"

"Now, yes. But I don't know what the future holds."

"I am imaging the future, Eric. Your future. My future . . . our future."

"How so, Poppa?"

"My vision of tomorrow is my son as the head of the family business."

"Poppa! What's this? Come on! What about Marvin and Ellen, or Ely? I am not the player you need!"

Haskell's words crashed down around them like thunderclaps: "I fired Marvin."

In the gravity of the moment Eric's jaw dropped, where it stayed. He was speechless. Finally, he asked with sarcasm and confusion, "The great seller and manager? Marvin? What?"

Haskell poured another Scotch for them both and downed his. *Is this my third or fourth today?* The heat from the liquor came back up his throat like venom. "That SOB was a conniving thief! He took kickbacks, thousands of dollars, from our suppliers—who knows what else! And the son of a bitch is running around on Hannahla."

Despite having more respect than to curse in front of his father, while his mouth was still agape, Eric threw in his second Scotch and chased it with, "Fuck!"

Haskell spoke as if issuing a commandment: "So I—the business—needs you and needs you now."

Eric wondered, *Has my whole life been but a preamble to this?* He locked eyes with his father, and by a mere uplift of one eyebrow and the hint of a conspiratorial smile, he agreed to the undertaking. Since he'd been at his father's knee, the timing for his joining the family business had yet to be determined. Now Eric understood and undertook the prospects.

"Dinner is ready! Please come in now," Molly called to them from the dining room.

Eric gently touched his father's hand. "I need time, Poppa. Give me a week or two, and I promise I will get back to you sooner."

"I know, now, who I need at my side," Haskell said.

CHAPTER 30

ALL OF THE ABOVE

In the three years since his college graduation, Eric had plunged into his assignments at a well-known architectural firm whose office, on the thirty-second floor, overlooked a large swath of uptown Manhattan. Raised by his father's old-world stories, he knew that this position exceeded his predecessors' wildest expectations about their New World fortune. What others took for seriousness was deep gratitude. He was sitting on top of the world, and he wasn't going to blow it.

As a child he would hide from his father's customers, pretending to be his father's reconnaissance officer, watching and eavesdropping if possible. His mission was to get intelligence for his father on how better to sell to them, and Haskell played along. Haskell pretended any tidbit from Eric was astounding and crucial to whatever sale was in the offing.

As an adult in his first grown-up position at the architecture firm, being outwardly unassuming masked Eric's inner determination to absorb and learn as much as possible as soon as possible. As if on a reconnaissance mission, he surveyed the landscape at work, and as he moved on, adopted what he saw as needed. If he saw how no one liked loud people, it was easy enough for him to adopt his father's even-tempered tone of voice. Each day was a master class.

He pitched in for the greater good but was careful not to overstep his place for those above him in the firm. So, he kept his distance and was deferential, letting others take the lead and credit. One of the advantages to this restraint was that it was interpreted as something more than it was—as a mystique. The firm's clients gravitated to his stillness and calm. Women did, as well. With his quiet demeanor, the longer he waited to speak, the more well regarded were his comments. He spoke sparingly, heeding the moral of the old saying, "You can be silent and maybe someone suspects you're not so smart, or you can open your mouth and prove it!"

Long-ingrained family scruples kept him from asking for help with what he could do himself. He was always willing to help others when the need arose. No task was too large or too humble for him. He was available when called upon, in part because he had nowhere much else to go or do, being single, and by nature "no" wasn't in his vocabulary. These courtesies, and his consistently honest efforts, accrued a reservoir of goodwill from his coworkers.

At work, his persona was a mystery. On the surface, he was quiet and handy in a pinch. And so it was that with time, this combination of reserve and helpfulness came to the notice of those in charge. Each year he had been rewarded with praise as well as an increase in salary and an incremental promotion.

It did not escape him that those moving faster in the firm were the son of one partner and the daughter of another. Eric could read the writing on the wall, as the son's and daughter's promotions came with successively larger offices—unlike his promotions. These heirs—which is how he regarded them—flaunted a sense of entitlement that spoke volumes about what he might expect, or not expect. Although the managing partner was a lifelong bachelor, the other two partners also had children, one a set of twins in high school, and the other a son already in college.

Eric had made his way up in the firm by keeping his head down. He enjoyed the upward trajectory and had not assumed his time at the firm was nearing its end. But his father's confrontation with Marvin presented an opportunity, the necessity for him to come to work at the family business. He felt assured he could decide within a week, and he found no excuse for procrastination.

In his marrow, he understood that this day would come, and this moment was now. To fulfill his father's vision, whether his entreaty was for health or otherwise, his father's needs would displace his own. Eric was inextricably bound to countless generations of family, landsmen, clan, neighbors, village, and religion. Who among the history of these from generations past could or would shirk their responsibilities? He had only to examine the unquestioning and undying devotion he felt for his parents to know his future was preset.

Yet at the architectural firm, he had laid down markers that established the proof of his maturity and earned self-worth. He was unsure he was, or might ever be, ready to surrender that. Every day he proved himself to the world. It wasn't as Poppa's heir; it was as Eric Brodsky. His inner voice questioned whether the time had truly come, if he was ready to abandon his autonomy.

Eric was searching for a tipping point, hoping it might be found in an exchange with the managing partner, Patrick Dillard. Dillard, a formal man always eager to appear easygoing, agreed to see him. At the risk of seeming obnoxious, Eric needed to clarify what his realistic prospects were for success at his current company versus the partners' offspring.

"Please, Eric, come on in," Dillard said when Eric came into his office. Eric took a seat opposite the older man.

"How can I help you, Eric?"

"I need, and I want, your honest advice."

"Of course!" Dillard chuckled. "Have I led you to expect anything else?"

"I expect fair dealing, which is what I have been privileged to enjoy here these last three years."

"And fair dealing is what we are all entitled to. Is there something troubling you?"

Eric could not think of a more diplomatic way to put it. "What are my opportunities in our firm for the future?"

"Have you not been rewarded for your hard work?"

"Yes. However, the daughter of one partner works hard here. The son of another partner works equally as hard. I am wondering whether the future here just belongs to family or whether I can compete equally. I harbor no ill will, because ironically, you know I, too, come from a family business."

Dillard seemed pained. "I meant to get to this sooner. Your work is excellent, and we voted you an increase in salary and we're working on a new title. I'm thinking assistant director of administration, so you can have your hands on a variety of projects and broaden your expertise. There is a future here for you, Eric."

"Thank you. Excuse me, but it's not my value that I question; I know my efforts have enriched the firm. I'm confident I've helped grow your company by successfully managing all the duties given me."

"And yet, I sense you are disturbed. By what? Has something happened?" Dillard asked.

"I have come to a crossroads. I hope you are able to answer a question directly. For me, given my background, it all boils down to this: Will I ever be offered an opportunity to have an equity position in the firm? What are my prospects, if any? I need to know sooner, rather than later."

Silence followed, "I see you are not as shy as I imagined. Coming from someone else, it would be impertinent. Is there some impetus to this?"

"My father's business needs me."

"And your prospects there?"

"Unlimited."

Dillard regarded him with more respect, and admiration, as he answered in a slow and deliberate manner. "The children of the partners come first—then everyone else. Does that answer your question? There is a place for you here, and you can continue to prosper here, for the long term. Here you will know that you made yourself a valuable component of our success."

After thinking, Eric replied, "Actually, no; I will only be what you allow me to be, and frankly, my ambition knows no limits."

"Can I ask you a question, Eric?"

"Sure."

"So, I am confused. Which are you: Shy Eric or ambitious Eric? I thought I had you pegged."

"Mr. Dillard, there's no conflict. I am and have been your student, your patient apprentice, your impatient journeyman, but I am a builder, not an architect, a builder of enterprises. I want to create my own, have my own enterprise. I don't want to always be handicapped."

"How can going to work at your father's business help you prove yourself?"

"My father cofounded a remarkably successful manufacturing and wholesale clothing business, and through it, generated an equally successful real estate company. They're on the verge of expanding both, and he is stretched in too many directions and asked me to help them grow to the next level."

"A dilemma to be jealous of! What's holding you back?"

"A sense of loyalty to this firm, to the opportunities I have received, appreciation for the sense of self you nurtured in me here."

"If you leave, you will not be disloyal," Dillard said benevolently and smiled. "You will not be a competitor because we are in different businesses. For some people, if they don't make their own destiny, they find themselves without one. If unbridled ambition motivates you, this place is not your calling. The best you can be here is an extremely high earner, but never an owner. Up until now, I thought it was enough for you to be paid fairly and have interesting work in an environment that values you. I speak for everybody when I say, I wish you would stay."

"If the situations were reversed, and you had a son or daughter at my father's company, what would you advise them?"

"I am me, not you. Honestly, I would advise you to return to where you belong, the family business. Rejoice that you acquired some seasoning at another business. And consider this: now, in the family business, you will have to work twice as hard to be considered worthy because you are the son. They will cut you no slack. Everything you do or don't do, all will be scrutinized. You will have to prove every day to every employee that you are not in your position for any reason other than you are the best qualified for it. Your efforts must overshadow any privilege for you to gain and retain the respect of the other workers. There is no substitute for sweat."

"Would you say that also applies or should apply to the partners' kids here?"

"If you keep asking me impertinent questions, I will not be sorry to see you go, Eric. As it is, you won't be going anywhere until you have satisfactorily rendered all your project commitments."

"I can wrap up my work within two weeks."

As Dillard reached to shake his hand, he said, "Answer my question, Eric."

"Which was?"

"So, which are you: Shy Eric or ambitious Eric? Silent Eric or shrewd Eric?"

Eric grasped Dillard's hand. "All of the above, sir."

CHAPTER 31

MOLLY

Eric would be joining the Friday evening Shabbat dinner. Molly reminded herself she should wear the charm bracelet he had given her for her birthday. As she cooked, she let the memories of the time when she was pregnant with Ely warm her.

She'd take Ellen and Eric to the local library for story hour. They were totally absorbed with each story read to them while she explored the card catalog and library stacks. Her library card was like gold to her. The staff welcomed the little ones and in time, all three children were library trained. Molly made it a point to go every week.

To her surprise, she was asked to volunteer two days a week at the library and agreed on the spot. She began shelving books and also kept up the receivables and assisted with planning the schedule. Finally, she was promoted to part-time customer support, aiding patrons behind the desk and finding books for them on the shelves. To her, everything was special about the experience, including being out of the house, as well as having a place to go where she was expected and respected. The staff's discussions made her feel like she was in college. As a volunteer librarian, she wasn't anyone's wife or mother; she was a professional, regarded seriously (and Haskell made sure she had the clothes to dress the part).

There was never a consideration for Molly to do more than volunteer in the library. To have taken a paid position was out of the question. Haskell's wife? Working?

As she smoothed the linens on the table, folded the napkins, and set the silver in place, she thought about her first job in America. She had dodged that predatory supervisor's advances and endured his lack of respect. She had lobbied for a promotion to bookkeeper and demonstrated for the other sewists the real opportunities they could create for themselves, even if they had to continue to watch for mistreatment at the hands of every boss.

After she and Haskell were married and had a baby on the way, Molly left her sweatshop job and found refuge in being a wife and mother, where she was safe and loved, and always respected.

She indulged herself in a philosophical reflection on how much revolved around the issue of respect, especially considering the impoverished circumstances from which she came.

Polishing the silver tea set to a mirrorlike shine, Molly considered that in their home, she was the family's epicenter. The home was her preserve, the focus of the stability and happiness of her family. Haskell imagined it was he, but who had birthed the children? There's no family without children! Who had created the warmth of a home to shelter them as they grew? Who had nurtured them, and shaped their daily lives to learn about the world and themselves?

Molly spent her quiet hours alone, often deep in thought. She would never share her secret feelings with her husband. Did she demonstrate respect for God and her husband? Yes, she did. She respected all those she loved. Did she demonstrate kindness? Yes, to her husband, whom she allowed to be the chief.

The table was set. The brisket was cooked and resting. *I am at the center, where I can allow my husband to believe that he is in charge, that he is the focus. Does he understand that he shares that exalted position?*

They had persevered through the Depression; those years, the 1920s and 1930s, had been hard. The war in 1941 was still more painful. Now living in a world of peace, during these postwar years Haskell's hard work had brought them stability. Their lives were on an upswing, the American dream was in their grasp. Molly gave thanks for their good fortune, for a family blessed with health and wealth. She gave thanks for Haskell, for the way he had brought the American dream to their door.

She had always admired Haskell's inner shine, his effortless ease with everyone he met, his charisma. Her own quiet thoughtfulness complemented and contrasted with his exuberance. On occasion, in private, she wearied of his confidence, and yes, his arrogance, but she hailed his brilliance in business. She thought, *Who wants a husband who could be pushed around? Even though his dedication to business was single-minded to a fault.*

She found the trade-off of wealth and security was suitable. He was her hero, even if over the years she had grown slightly less interested in his revolving parade of stories that featured him in starring roles. She provided an audience for him, a supporting player in their family drama at best, or at worst, an invisible understudy.

On any given day, her silent parade of stories were of the shopping, food preparation and service, observance of Shabbat, laundry, dishes, mending, child-rearing, and household maintenance, the countless quiet and invisible transactions and preparations, all done without wages or acknowledgment.

That's OK, she thought. *I am not motivated by money. My value transcends money. I make generations.* She smiled as she thought of Ellen, Eric, and Ely as her greatest achievements. Ellen, whose independent nature and strong will had shown early. Molly had encouraged her, knowing that a life like her own would never have been enough.

Eric had been her adventurer, her wild child full of joy. He would take on whatever the world presented to him.

And Ely, her dear, loving boy, who had bridged easily between his siblings, keeping the peace when they squabbled, unusually aware even as a toddler of what they needed.

Yes, she had also built on the riches America had brought to her door.

Molly relaxed with a cup of tea in the quiet, letting her thoughts drift. *What is the meaning of the phrase, "What makes a man?" I know what makes a man*, she asked and answered herself with a chuckle. *A woman makes a man. Is there a man conceived without a mother, without grandmother, aunt, sister, cousin, wife, daughter, friend, coworker? Is there a man who can succeed without his helpmate?*

Should we also not ask, "What makes a woman?" This brought her to thinking, *What made me? I am practical, and my ambitions have been realistic: to love and be loved, to care and be cared for. To make my support of whomever I love a constant.*

Measuring where she came from and the circumstances in which she now found herself, she judged herself fortunate to have achieved her ambitions for herself and her family. As her grandmother said in Yiddish, "Kinder, gezunt un gelt is a shaine veldt [Children, health, and treasure make a beautiful world]."

CHAPTER 32

GRACE

Eric had his own thoughts that morning as he braced himself for Shabbat dinner at his parents' home. He thought, *They are not going to like this turn of affairs.* Still, he would do his best.

At lunch, he raced to the Diamond District to a jeweler from the old country with a stall in lower Manhattan who had become what the Brodskys thought of as their family jeweler. Shimon was both kind and honest. In college, Eric had bought a charm bracelet for his mother's birthday, initiating an annual tradition of getting a new charm for her birthdays and Mother's Day. Today wasn't one of those events, but it would, however, be an important occasion.

It was impossible for him resist preparing to use his parents' own words, as his father told him after college, "Go out in the world, get your own experience, be your own man."

Eric mulled over Poppa's advice. *Isn't loving someone of my own choice an extension of Poppa's counsel? I must be who I am,* he thought, *at whatever cost. As an American, I have come to enjoy the friendship of a larger, non-Jewish world. This will be my world, not the world of my father.*

Haskell had also said to him, more than once, "The love of a good woman is above all. The secret to a happy life is finding the person who will love you forever." Wasn't his mother known to say,

"Whosoever will be your chosen companion will be welcome in our home"?

He trusted them; they had faith in him. He believed in himself, and now, that trust would be evaluated.

He hoped to speak with Ellen first and get her input. She was still reeling since her husband had been exposed as a cheater at home and at work.

Eric wasted no time after his arrival giving his mother the new charm for her bracelet, which she was wearing. This one was a gold heart with a small ruby. He was reminded of the Biblical proverb, "A wife of noble character, who can find? She is far more precious than rubies."

"What is the occasion?" Molly asked with delight.

"I don't need an occasion to give you anything, Momma. I love you."

Haskell walked out of the room for a moment, giving Molly a few moments with Eric.

"Your father's doctor's visit did not go well," she whispered. "He said Haskell was under excessive pressure and needed less aggravation and had to change his diet."

Eric chuckled. "You don't expect him to slow down, do you?"

"Maybe not, but this makes it a very good time for you to join the company, doesn't it?" Molly smiled at her co-conspirator.

Eric decided to ease his father into thinking he was coming onboard to prove himself. To garner his respect, he'd downplay his motivation to relieve his father of some of the aggravation that weighed on him. This move was equal parts what he should do, and what he had to do, for both Haskell and him.

Dinner progressed through the small talk of the day until they laid their forks down.

"So, let's talk," Haskell said. "You have a lot to learn and understand about how we run the firm, and who's who. I am not going anywhere, and Hannahla—uh, Ellen—who's got seven years of on-the-job training, has worked very hard. From my point of view, she has earned every inch of authority she has, and she deserves to use it. I want you to work closely with her and learn. I only advance those who earn a promotion. Don't expect a picnic. You're not the boss yet."

This is the easy part, Eric thought. "Poppa, I want no handouts like the partners I worked for gave their kids. I want to earn my keep. Assign me the toughest projects. I've been thinking about this: give me your three or four toughest issues! First, I want to manage the audit of Marvin's embezzlement. It would be helpful if Ellen were there. She has accounting skills, and having her go through the process will allow her to confront the truth of her husband. Hopefully, it may help her recover from his deceit."

Haskell nodded.

"Second, since we have invested and bought buildings and managed them, I would like to take over the real estate receivables and manage the assets there."

My son knows architecture; he will know what I don't know about managing those buildings, Haskell thought.

"Third, I want to try my hand at bringing back lost customers. Fourth, since I've worked on international projects, I would like to assume responsibility for any international organization here. My goal is to earn your respect as if I were a stranger to you. I want you to be proud of my work separate and apart from being your son."

Haskell appraised his son's offer. "As to these four things you would like to take on: one, I want the Ellen-Marvin soap opera over as soon as possible. I appreciate your recognizing that problem; find every penny that thief took from us. Two, with your background, you can jump into real estate work without difficulty. Three, as for recovering lost customers, if anyone can, you can! Fourth, as for the rest of the world, help yourself!"

They both smiled. Eric reached out to his father and shook his hand.

Haskell could not curb his excitement. "There's more to be done. There are other delicate issues I will bring you up-to-date on. For example, when we bought the building next door, we inherited the janitor. He thinks he's the building manager; please replace him with someone more energetic.

"As for the trade, we need to improve our sourcing and lower the cost of goods, without sacrificing quality. I could use someone to work through these things with me." Haskell sat back with a sigh of satisfaction.

Molly cleared the table and reset it for dessert. Eric had waited, holding back his news until the meal was finished.

"Momma, you taught Hannah and Ely and me to respect each other and to respect you and Poppa," he began. "That might have been your first lesson for us. Poppa, you always said the most important thing is to find the right woman, a woman who will love you forever. Both of you told me to learn to stand on my own two feet, to fight for what is right, to combat religious and racial discrimination. In shul, in our synagogue, we are shown to love our fellow man, to pursue justice, to be righteous. These are your ideals, and mine. But I don't need religion to tell me right from wrong, love from hate, good from bad. I am judge enough."

His parents listened closely, digesting it all.

After pausing, he continued, "Momma, Poppa, I've met the girl. She is everything to me."

Molly brightened. "How wonderful! Tell us more."

"I need to ask you: If she had a lisp, would you mind?"

"No, of course not."

"If she were very short, would it matter?"

"No."

"If she were rich or poor, would it make a difference?"

Hesitation, then, "No."

"If she had a limp, would that be terrible?"

"No."

"If she couldn't have children, could you love her all the same?"

At this, Molly let out a whimper.

"Don't worry, Momma," Eric said. "She is beautiful, healthy, from a family of means, and nothing at all is wrong with her."

Haskell said emphatically, "My son, we trust your judgment."

"Thank you, Poppa. Because she is Asian American."

Silence filled the room.

"What is that?" Molly asked, confused.

"Do you remember when I went to Asia for the architecture firm? My coordination partner, Mr. Soong, introduced me to his daughter when she came to visit us at the office. We became friends, and for me it was love at first sight. Her name is Grace, and she recently graduated from college."

Molly and Haskell sat, stone-faced.

Molly spoke first. "It's nice you're in love. You're not saying you want to marry her, right?"

"Mother, I *do* want to marry her. I want you to want what I want. She is who I need in my life. I see her as a unique person. I hope you will feel as I do."

Following a long pause, Eric resumed speaking with a quiet intensity. "Poppa, you always said the most important thing is love. There's nothing at all wrong with being in love with someone not from the same clan. We are all of one God. This is America, land of freedom and opportunity; isn't that what brought you to America?"

Eric's aim was true. Haskell sat, deep in his own thoughts.

Molly roused herself from her surprise. She did a quick check on what she did believe: yes, she had known many different people, all sizes and flavors, and it didn't matter. Her potential daughter-in-law's background was not belittling of her own beliefs or history. She would be no less of herself. *Eric is right, there's no shame.*

Molly gazed at her poker-faced husband, drew a deep breath, and closed her eyes. She turned to her son, touched his hand, and peered into his eyes, saying, "I need to meet her."

Eric wrapped his mother in his arms and kissed her cheek.

Molly's loving kindness amazed Haskell, prompting him to think, *I hope she will bring kindness to us all. I would never have expected this. I do not know my wife as I imagined. In the old world, there weren't so many places to go to, so you stayed in your village, met people from other towns, none too far away, and we held fast to our traditions. In the New World, people move—there's my older brother Label, farming in Indiana far from us. If we didn't accept her, Eric could get angry and move away. I have no kids to spare. I am not Abraham; I will not sacrifice my son on an altar of bigotry.* He checked himself, cleared his throat, and said, "I need to meet her, too, and soon."

Eric stretched out his other arm to encompass his father, who could not help but also shed tears.

CHAPTER 33

ERIC'S LAST ARCHITECTURE DAY

On his last day, Eric enjoyed a parting lesson from Mr. Dillard. The young man thanked the senior partner for the career opportunities he was given and offered to help with any transitional issues. Mr. Dillard sat at the head of the conference table, looked into his eyes, and said, "Eric, bonuses are ordinarily a year-end disbursement. While it is not customary to do so, the firm's managers have directed me to award a bonus reflecting your contribution this year to date."

"Thank you; I appreciate the consideration. May I ask to what I owe this departure from practice?"

"You have consistently gone above and beyond, and your discretion and judgment have impressed us. We strive to conduct business in a manner that rewards results, including enhancing our reputation. You have done all these things. While we are sorry to see you go, the circumstances speak for themselves. Personally, I will miss you."

Mr. Dillard paused and nodded toward Eric. "Call me for lunch when you have made your mark; I want to hear all about it! And when your real estate business needs an architect, we hope you'll call us."

He stood and withdrew an envelope from his breast pocket and handed it to Eric.

"Go home early. That's my last order." They shook hands warmly as Eric turned to leave.

Eric thought Dillard's gesture of generosity, coupled with the pitch for a future business collaboration, was the sign of a successful businessperson. He promised himself he would remember it in the future.

Eric pushed open the glass doors to the street and looked up at the building where he had spent the past few years. A bright, sunny New York afternoon lit up the windows all the way to the top like a blessing, and the street was quiet for these moments before the close of the workday. He turned and signaled for a cab, patting the envelope in his pocket.

My father was right to urge me to risk taking my first job elsewhere, not in the family business where I would be loved and protected, but where I could learn for myself our five-generation motto: "The harder you work, the luckier you get." I can stand before my parents, knowing I can succeed in an independent business environment, that I am my own man.

On the way home, he thought of what a striking change it would be to spend his days with his sister and younger brother, as well as his father. Each relationship, and the four of them working together as a team, would need to be sensitive to each other's needs as they established their new rhythms. It would take patience to avoid stepping on anyone's toes.

Then he remembered the envelope. He smiled as he saw the figure of $2,000, and thought, *This is the perfect amount for an engagement ring!*

From his apartment, he dialed the office. "Hello, Sandra. Please let me speak to my sister."

Ellen picked up immediately. "Welcome onboard, Eric. I am going to need your help very much, more than you know. We're operating at capacity and expanding simultaneously. There's so much to do and so much we must discuss. The timing couldn't have been better. Are you ready?"

"I'm all yours," he responded.

"I've arranged for you to take the office directly next to mine. Can you hit the pavement running first thing Monday morning? Rest up over the weekend because you are going to work harder than you ever have. Dad's going to give you keys over the weekend." In an even tone that he recognized meant acceptance, she concluded, "I heard about Grace. I want to meet her as soon as possible."

He had never loved Ellen more.

CHAPTER 34

THE DREAM COMES TRUE

Eric arrived at the Abraham & Brodsky offices Monday at 7:45 a.m. With the new key in his hand, he opened the door.

"Surprise, surprise," everyone called out. Ellen, Ely, and Sandra had orchestrated a welcome party with bagels, lox, cream cheese, and coffee.

Ely had bought everything, and boasted, "We know you like a book! You thought you could beat us in on your first day! Not a chance! This is a new family competition, and it's going to be fun. Do you remember how you used to get up early every Saturday morning to go with Dad to work while Ellen and I slept? Those days are over—we're the early birds now, and you have a lot of catching up to do!"

The four celebrated as if it were a homecoming. Sandra seemed exhilarated, whispering conspiratorially to him, "You're very much needed!"

Ellen asked Ely to start a briefing with Eric. Everyone's long-awaited dream began. They sat in Ely's office, sketching out the operations and relevant personalities.

Eric was determined to unearth all of Marvin's financial improprieties, protective of his older sister, and deferential to their father. Ely promised, "You will have my total commitment. Our generation is all set to build our company into the largest clothing company in America."

Later, as he passed Ellen's office, she waved to him as she spoke with a client on the telephone.

He sat in his new office for a few minutes, trying to find the word—"utilitarian"—to encapsulate the simplicity of Abraham & Haskell's offices. *We need new telephones and better typewriters*, he thought. *We have serious upgrades to plan.*

His phone rang. *Ah, my first call, it's beginning. Let's go, let's go.* "Hello, this is Eric."

"I know, I know. It's Ellen. I called you on the intercom; it's a different ring than direct or transferred outside calls. Would you please come into my office?"

Ellen's office had belonged to their father, who had moved into Uncle Abe's old office so Ellen could have more space. She sat in one of the two nail-studded armchairs in the alcove, and Eric sat in the other. He looked around at the additions and changes Ellen had made to the office. The room seemed brighter. It had been painted, the shelves on the credenza cleared, and a new blue and gray Oriental rug added that lifted the room to match Ellen's energy.

She spoke in a clear voice. "You and I have much work to do. I know you're not a beginner. It was better for you and all of us that you were able to get experience and tasted success somewhere else first. I am glad I am rid of the shitty garment-district job I had before I came here." She smiled.

"The main lesson I have learned in the business world is that it's all about timing. It's key. Business, and life, are like yeast: you must nurture it, and it takes time. I feel confident you will be able to manage because I need to step aside from my job for a while. With Marvin gone, it is a new season for me now. I have a different purpose, and it's time for me to have my turn, to heal; to mourn;

to cast away; and a time to love. I've decided to take a six-month sabbatical."

Eric was surprised to hear that she was stepping away, giving up so easily. This was not her! She was the eldest, and he had been looking forward to the competition she would offer.

She plowed ahead of his confusion. "For the next week or two, you and I will be at it every day for as much as you can take. It will not be stress-free. But you can do it. You must work harder than you ever have. You, Dad, and Ely are the new bosses. I even have a name for you: I will call you the tripod! A tripod is stable and self-supporting. The three of you will assure that the business will be stable, and become more prosperous."

"Why? Poppa brags that you have made this company the success it is!"

"I have tried to have it all. I'm now a woman going through a divorce with a young child, who is my priority now. I cannot have it all and do it all well. Perhaps I can have it all, but just not at the same time. I don't want to compromise every area of my existence. The drama with Marvin, the disappointment, my shame, and my pain are huge distractions. Ben also needs extra attention to adapt to life without his father. I want to take six months off to clear it all away."

"Over my seven years here, I have acquired the skills to run this company around the clock. I've done so while being a wife and mother and now, without a husband."

Ellen sighed. "I need time. Remember I said the paramount lesson may be timing? It is time for me to take a break. I've earned it.

"So, here is the scenario: we work together until you get up to snuff on every issue of this job. I won't be easy on you, but you will get it. The sooner you absorb it, the sooner I can go take care of myself. You have two weeks, maximum. OK? Got it? I need you to say yes. Ben needs me. I need to unhook here. Divorce is messy, and I have meetings with my lawyer and an accountant going through our personal finances."

Eric nodded and leaned over to take his sister's hand, then enveloped her in a hug that brought them both to tears. She held him at arm's length, and her eyes were soft as she told him, "Nothing is as it appears to be, nor is it otherwise. That's Dad's take on it. I know this is not what you expected. In business—as in life—expect the unexpected."

"OK. Let's get started! Until you leave, you're the boss, and I'm your pupil. What do you have to do today? Teach me from that."

An hour passed while they worked, and then Haskell called Ellen's office. "Dad wants you in his office," she told Eric. "When you're done, come back."

He stepped into his father's office and with a salute, said, "Ah, Mr. Brodsky, good day! Private Brodsky reporting for duty, sir!"

Haskell returned the salute, smiled, and said, "At ease, Private. Welcome back, my son. It's been a long time since we worked together. This is quite a happy day for me. You have much to learn. Let's get to it."

They settled at Haskell's desk. "I am pleased that Hannah, I mean, Ellen is guiding your education," Haskell said. "However, starting with her, and with everyone, please know that a humble approach will never fail you. The most important words might be, 'What do you think?' Here, please understand, you cannot be a leader by command. You can only lead by example. There is nothing that is not earned or acquired carefully.

"Whatever obstacles you encounter, be assured you are never without resources; I count myself foremost among the assets we have here. Ellen is indispensable, and Ely's energy drives us all."

Haskell continued, "All power comes from proof of integrity. The power I have here comes from the trust people have in me. Everyone knows if I say I can do something, I will. And I will do it honestly. My word is my bond." He added, "And sales ability, of course, is a critical part of our success; you inherited this from a long line."

Seeing he had made his point, Haskell unlocked his lower-right desk drawer and withdrew a four-inch binder that he placed on his blotter. He opened it to a page that had a paperclip attached to it and turned it to face Eric. "What do you see?" he asked.

Ely focused on the map in front of him and said, "China."

"Yes, son. I have seen the writing on the wall, and I am convinced we can find materials and markets in this undeveloped country that will catapult our business beyond anything we have done yet."

"Are you ready to tell me how?"

"Between the 1920s and 1940s, China fought Japan, a civil war, a world war, and another civil war—and now is drowning in a war with Korea. They are communist now, but they also are in tatters. They have natural resources and are desperately poor. When they stop fighting in Korea, they will be even poorer and more in need of manufacturers and clothes. They confiscate capital, but do you think the government is going to build businesses? Their rulers will hoard their riches like all other regimes. Their people will starve until they can get foreign capital to begin factories. I am keeping everything I come across about China as a sales market and manufacturing site. It may not be now, or soon, but one day China will awaken, and they will want to catch up, and I want to be in on the ground floor."

Haskell tossed bound reports and trade magazines onto the binder as it lay open on his desk. "We need to study shipping more. We will start with Taiwan or Hong Kong, both good places for factories and labor. You said Grace's family is Taiwanese, and I am thinking this union might be bashert [meant to be]!

"Which of the four of us have to learn Chinese?"

"When the time comes, you will want to learn Chinese. One last thing: when you confer with Ely, do everyone a favor and don't treat him like your kid brother. I didn't like it when your Uncle Abe did that to me. I don't want a repetition of that. Now go, learn from your brilliant sister how she's almost single-handedly responsible for our recent biggest sales and leases."

Ellen and Eric, with assistance from Ely, worked diligently for the next ten days, including the weekend. Both brothers were amazed at the depth and breadth of their sister's sales knowledge: customers; cash flow; accounts receivable; aging summaries; the pros and cons of issues in production, inventory, and personnel; and their real estate business. She had an encyclopedic knowledge of each customer, complete with a running commentary of their liquidity and their level of difficulty. She had developed a custom-ized charm offensive for each customer: a semiannual visit, lunch or dinner on the house, drinks somewhere with a view or in a nice hotel, holiday baskets. Her special touches solidified customer loyalty to Abraham & Haskell.

On the afternoon of the tenth day, Haskell, Ellen, Eric, and Ely went to Gina's restaurant for a farewell lunch. Haskell stood up, paper cup in hand, filled with 7UP, and said, "May my Hannahla—our Ellen—have a healing and fulfilling sabbatical and come back to work soon!"

Everyone cheered softly, including Gina. Ellen lifted her glass and toasted him in return. "I will miss work, and all of you, and hope we will see each other often. As you and Momma taught me, in the words of Hillel, 'If I am not for myself, who will be for me?'

And to Eric and Ely: thank you from the bottom of my heart for your support. I love you all very much. Good luck and success! Be smart and listen to Dad!"

Haskell turned to Gina. "Let's not forget to thank Gina, for the best pizza in Manhattan!"

CHAPTER 35

GRACE COMES TO CALL

The taxi pulled up to the Central Park apartment. "Grace, my love, please don't be nervous. My parents are not going to eat you alive. They are nice people. Mom is more nervous than you are. She is wonderful to all three of us, but tougher than my father. She may ask a lot of questions. Just be your beautiful self and the Grace I love."

"Eric, I know it will be fine, but why am I trembling? I can't believe how calm you were when we met my parents for lunch last Sunday. You were great. They loved you."

"Try to calm down, sweetheart. My parents will love you, too."

The building concierge called up his parents' apartment to announce them and then directed them to the elevator. Eric squeezed Grace's hand.

"Momma, Poppa, let me introduce you to Grace, my . . . let me see . . . for now, my girlfriend. Grace, this is my mother, Molly, and my father, Haskell. Be nice to him. He is my boss." His humor eased the awkwardness of the moment.

Molly extended her hand to Grace. "Welcome to our home, Grace. Please call us by our first names."

Haskell swept his hand toward the two-tiered cocktail cart laid with hors d'oeuvres beside decanters of liquor. "But first, a drink! What will you have, Grace?"

"What is everyone else having?" Grace asked.

"I'm having a Scotch. I'm pretty sure Eric will head for a beer from the refrigerator and put the kettle on for Molly, who is a big tea drinker."

Grace said, "Then it's a Scotch for me." Haskell grinned. *Atta, girl! The best answer.*

Molly led Grace to the sofa. "Come sit next to me and tell me all about yourself."

"Thank you," Grace hesitated, "Molly."

They nibbled on appetizers as Grace looked around the room. "What a lovely apartment! You have made a lovely home."

Eric cleared his throat and said, "I am so glad that we are here tonight for dinner and for you to meet Grace. She was so nervous. Can you believe that? Frightened to meet my gentle mom and dad; it's a puzzle."

Molly followed immediately by turning to Grace and gently touching her hand. "Grace, darling," she began, "you could not be as nervous as me. Imagine! You are the first young woman that Eric has ever introduced us to!"

Grace smiled and lowered her eyes in respect for what she heard. This did not go unnoticed by Haskell, who recognized poise when he saw it.

"Tell us about yourself," Haskell suggested.

"Poppa, this is not an interview!" Eric said.

"Grace, tell us about your work. I am always interested in anyone's work stories, including yours. I'm not prying; I'm curious. Eric said that you are in finance. What do you do? What do you want to do?"

Grace noticed that Haskell had diverted the attention from her family and background to a more neutral subject.

Eric watched her sizing up his father. He was pleased she was no longer nervous and had warmed to his parents already. She gave him a look that said, *You needn't be concerned. I can do this. I am ready.*

Eric nodded once and relaxed in his chair so she could have the floor. Molly smiled at Haskell, and both could see the mutual respect Eric and Grace demonstrated for each other.

"Since college, I've worked in the bonds department of Morgan, Ranch & Cohen, where I evaluate the merits of potential investments for my firm," Grace said. "I'm an analyst. Two years ago, I graduated Phi Beta Kappa from Columbia, where I studied business."

Grace decided to address the unspoken questions about her parents directly. "I am an only child; both of my parents are natives of Taiwan. My father is an architect for a Taipei—that is the capital of Taiwan—construction company that opened a New York office right after the war. Because of his fluency in English, he was chosen to be the first person to be sent to the New York office. We all came together in 1945, when I was seventeen. My father insisted that the company provide my mother and me with an English tutor in Taiwan before we moved here, where we studied English for three months, and a tutor for us here as soon as we arrived.

"My mother and I studied English day and night, which allowed me to finish my high school senior year here on time. My mother is fluent in English now. Oh, did I mention I live with my parents? One thing my parents say is that they will never go back to Taiwan. When I graduated, I applied to become an American citizen. My mother is considering it, too. She's a volunteer with the Red Cross. She schedules appointments for people to donate blood."

Grace took a breath and continued. "My father's office is close to mine, and one day he asked me to come over for lunch to discuss construction bonds. We had started the discussion in his office when Eric brought in some blueprints. He seemed curious about my business and lingered. I thought he was handsome and smart, so I was thrilled that he called my father the next day to ask if he could call me. My parents don't care if he's Jewish because they're atheists, and they want what I want."

That last phrase registered with Haskell.

With perfect timing, Molly leaned forward. "Are you hungry? Come, let me feed you."

CHAPTER 36

ASIA AWAITS

Haskell could not believe his good luck. Eric brought Grace into their lives, and two weeks later at their Shabbat dinner, all they talked about was their opportunity in Taiwan. Grace had a head for significant business, not the kind you get from book learning. For Molly, it was a joy to watch the eye-to-eye conversations among the three of them, Haskell, Grace, and Eric filled with laughter between serious discussions of economics and politics.

The next week, Haskell asked Molly if it was all right to invite Grace to visit them on the next Sunday afternoon so he could pick her brain some more. He was fueled by his rapid understanding of Asian business and wanted to have another in-depth conversation with her.

"My dear husband, you are shameless! Lucky for you, I am happy to have her join us again."

Once Grace was there, Haskell leveled with her. "I am fascinated by the potential for trade in Asia," he said. "Please forgive me if I am overstepping my bounds here, but could you help me locate potential clothing factories that manufacture suits in Taiwan? I ask you not to be insulted by my offer to pay you for your help."

"You cannot pay me in money," she said. "I am in love with your son. If I'm around, I am going to help him grow the family business anywhere in the world."

For a week, Haskell replayed that sentence over and over in his mind: *I am going to help him grow the family business anywhere in the world.* Within ten days, Haskell had a list. Grace started researching factories in Taiwan and laying the groundwork for overseas visits. She also gave him the name and contact information of her English tutor in Taipei to use as a translator there.

Haskell looked to the heavens and thanked God for Grace.

Although it was logical to send Eric to Taiwan, to everyone's surprise he sent Ely. The young man needed some international seasoning to bring him up to Eric's level.

Ten days passed. "Hello, hello, Eric, can you hear me? The connection is not great."

"Yes, I can, Ely. Give me some good news."

Ely, normally a quiet young man, shouted, "Thank God I had Grace's tutor to translate! Things are moving fast. Listen to this: suits that cost us twenty-two dollars in Vineland, New Jersey, and nineteen dollars in Pottsville, Pennsylvania, are only eleven dollars here on average, and that's without negotiating—plus shipping!"

"How is the tailoring?"

"Better than I expected. I went to two of the three Taipei factories so far, gave them the test suit patterns, and each factory made a sample overnight. So far, they don't know I am visiting three factories, which will be good when it is time for Poppa to negotiate."

"Ely, I knew you'd give us a head start! Tell me more."

"I checked the tailoring details and feel sure either of these factories can deliver every request we make, like hand stitching the lapels and flap pockets, making two inside breast pockets, et cetera. They can produce prototypes overnight that appear acceptable to exceptionally good. Tomorrow I will go to the last factory. I leave in two and a half days."

"Keep up the pace! Excellent job! I can't wait to tell Grace and Haskell. Thank you."

It took Ely more than a day of air travel to return to the States, and Haskell and Eric joined him for lunch at Gina's to review the details of his trip.

Eric marveled at their good fortune, and his father's idea to seek international suppliers.

"Your studies at CCNY are serving you well, Ely." Haskell beamed with pride.

"That's true, Pop. There are ways I'm applying my courses to this opportunity in ways I haven't been able to in the company. I've profiled the companies, built relationships with them, and I've got three bids in my pocket!"

Eric gave his brother a playful shove. "You didn't know you could do it, but we did! Who knows what you'll accomplish next."

Gina came by with a trio of cannoli for them. "Sounds like beshert to me."

"How does Gina know Yiddish?" The four burst into laughter.

CHAPTER 37

ANTHONY DELIVERS
A PROPOSAL

Anthony buzzed on the intercom and asked to talk to Eric at the end of the day. In the three years since Gina's son had come onboard as assistant sales director, he had become the sales director and gotten married to Shirley. They had all gone to the interfaith wedding at Brooklyn's Flatbush Reform Temple, and it was apparent to all that the traditions of the Italians and the Jews were synonymous. Molly danced with Anthony; Haskell had a dance with Gina.

As for the tikkun olam for Abe, a donation had been made in honor of Abe Brodsky; it was now all history.

At five o'clock, Anthony sat down in Eric's s office. "We have always been straight with each other," he said. "Let me come to the point: Shirley's family, the ones with the investment group, as they call it, approached me. They want to go straight. They want to give up their family business and become legitimate."

"That's an exceptionally clever idea. I'm curious how this came about."

Anthony hunched over his legs and interlaced his fingers. He confided, "All the big bosses are doing it. They are going into the casino and hotel business, trucking, local oil delivery, and even fancy Italian restaurants."

Eric read the newspaper every day. Cautiously, he inquired, "So tell me, Anthony, does the Senate's investigation with Kefauver have anything to do with this? It's a smart move. They should have done it years ago."

Anthony remained on course. "All of the Levy families on Shirley's side want to go into real estate investments."

Eric suspected what was coming.

"They understand that your family owns five buildings on Fifth Avenue. They would like to buy them, tear the buildings down, and build a thirty-story tower."

Eric thought his father needed to be present for this conversation, but this was what was happening, and he wasn't going to derail the momentum. He pointed out, "Those buildings do not belong to me. They belong to our entire family. And of course, in the end, my dad will make the final decision."

"But does it sound like something you and your family would be interested in?"

"In fact, about two years ago—you must've been here about a year then—we had an offer; this was right before I came to work at the company. Their offer was different from your group's. They invited us to join them as equal partners. Five buildings, five million dollars for the family. The entire responsibility for the construction and any related issues would be theirs, although the family would be consulted on every issue. In the end, we decided that the property was even more valuable than that."

"Would you have agreed if their proposal was six million?"

"Anthony, like I said, it's not up to me. I am in the men's clothing business."

"I ask your permission to approach your father. May I have your blessing?"

"Only because it's you."

"Don't worry. I am more loyal to you than to Shirley's Levy cousins."

I like Anthony, but is that true? Eric stood and ended the meeting.

Later that afternoon, Eric walked into Haskell's office. "We need to discuss something," he said.

"Always!" Haskell said with a smile.

"OK, this is serious. Anthony confided in me about something that seemed like an opportunity, but I can't begin to think it through without you. He said the investment guys, the Levys, his wife, Shirley's, family branch that dealt with Uncle Abe, want to go straight. They want to start or join legitimate businesses."

"Good luck to them," Haskell said with studied indifference.

"They want to go into the real estate business."

"Good luck to them," he repeated.

"They want to buy our buildings for something above five million dollars, tear them down, and build a skyscraper."

Haskell sat back deeply in his chair. He put his hands out in front of him, his fingers spread on both hands, tenting each other.

Haskell held up his hands. "The world," he said and indicated with his fingers, "is interconnected. There is no escaping cause and effect. My father said, 'You lie down with dogs, you wake up with fleas.' So, no, no, we don't, we won't do business with those people. They cannot change. Their needs are not our needs. They will see an opportunity for a quick profit, take it, and disappear. We bought those five buildings for about a million and a half, or less. In just shy of five years, their value has quadrupled. What we own is priceless. Manhattan is an island. The land is limited. Our property may be worth fifty million dollars in ten years. We are successful enough. When we enter the Asia supply market, I expect us to enjoy additional success. Most important, we can never do business with those people; you cannot lower your standards for money." Shaking his finger, he said, "Remember this."

Eric was momentarily embarrassed that he had even considered the proposal.

Haskell caught his son's furrowed brow and said, "And if we ever want to, we can do that tower project by ourselves. We never, never want partners. Not now, not ever! You tell Anthony, 'Thanks, but no thanks.' No matter how many times or ways he asks you, you say only these four words: 'Thanks, but no thanks.' You cannot give those people an inch—I don't mean Anthony, I mean the Levys. Don't leave any wiggle room. Show them we have full confidence in ourselves. Do it with a smile, and stand tall. They'll get the message."

"Yes, sir."

CHAPTER 38

GRACE GETS A COMMITMENT

Grace and Eric had managed to charm each other's families. Her parents looked the other way when one night she took a garment bag with her to go out with Eric. Her mother asked, "What's in the bag?" and Grace said, simply, "Clothes for work tomorrow." Her mother viewed Grace with new respect: *My daughter is a grown woman, now twenty-five years old. It is her life, and all I want is for her to be happy. I could not hope for anything more.*

In Eric's apartment, the two lovers sat around the kitchen table, sharing a dinner they had prepared together, an act of intimacy they relished even though both were tired from their workday.

"Are you bored, Grace?"

"A little. Why? What do you propose?"

Eric dropped from his chair to his knee, ripped a small box from under the table where he had taped it, and said, "I propose you marry me!"

Grace erupted in laughter. "What else have you got taped under there?" She joined him on the floor, kissing him wildly until he gasped, "Would you look in the box already!"

"I'm not marrying the ring! I'm marrying you! Now let me see it! I can't wait."

Frankly, it had never occurred to him that Grace would say no.

On her knees with him, Grace looked at the ring as if it was a mirage and collapsed into tears.

Hang on! Eric thought. *Here's a woman laughing one moment and crying the next. Love is crazy.*

Grace called her parents right away. They heard shrieks of joy echo through the phone.

The next day, Eric called his parents. "I have good news, great news, but I am not going to tell you until I see you."

"You have five minutes to get here!" Molly ordered.

At noon, Grace and Eric appeared at the apartment door and it took only a fraction of a second for Molly to look at Grace's face and blurt out, "I knew it!"

Grace held up her left hand for them to see the proof. Haskell looked relieved. "Who's got champagne?" he asked. He had grown to care about Grace, and they formed a cluster and hugged each other.

Ely came in and offered toasts. Molly called Ellen, who arrived with Ben, still too young to understand. Still, he laughed because everyone around him was so happy.

As Eric watched Molly, Ellen, and Grace chatter over the ring, he warmed at the thought that Ellen and Grace would be close, and that Molly had welcomed her so warmly. It felt like Grace rounded out the family. In some odd way, she completed them.

CHAPTER 39

THE DEBRIEFING

Haskell had been deliberate in grooming his children to succeed. He was precise in his compliments, criticism, and delegation of authority. For him, it was a vote of his confidence in Eric (and Grace) that he left the planning of the Taipei trip in their hands.

He fed Ely a steadily increasing diet of business experiences and challenges, testing but not overwhelming him. He considered Ely's success a direct reflection of himself, and what Haskell had learned with his first two children, he applied to Ely.

He asked his younger son to lead the debriefing meeting of his trip to Taipei. Ely was a numbers person; everything was a number, a statistic, a percentage, an addition, or subtraction. Haskell liked this style, for he was always good with figures himself; it had been his best subject in school.

The younger brother talked to his father and Eric about his trip. He shared the pros and cons of each of the three factories. These production facilities were all acceptable. The differences were to be weighed. A key decision hung in the balance.

Ely detailed and compared the state of the equipment of every factory, the merits of the owners and manager, the size and age of the business, and of course, their sample output, which he displayed.

The three examined the suits closely. Then they discussed the relative merits of the factories and their samples.

"What is your verdict?" Ely asked Haskell.

"Let me begin by telling you that I am impressed with how well you pulled this trip off. You have a real talent for this. But I knew I could rely on you. You are my scout, and no endeavor is successful without at least one scout.

"Verdict? As to which company we should move ahead with, I am going to take some time later to think this through myself.

"But let's be sober about our enormous opportunity, move forward slowly, and quietly. This does not leave this office. Eric, you tell Grace that, too, OK?

"I want to consider sending Ely to Taipei to be there for the launch. We must have someone knowledgeable to watch quality production, packing, and shipping. All those are essential. I want eyes and ears on the ground, at least at the outset. Minimize risk."

"It's a go?" Eric asked.

Haskell held up his palm. "This cannot be done as is. It must be executed to perfection. We are not going to do anything half-assed. It seems clear and vital that we find two or three bilingual men or women. They will be able to communicate your instructions to our suppliers in Asia. Grace or Grace's father could help us locate them; I think a man and a woman would be useful. Now, if you'll excuse me, I need time to myself."

Eric and Ely stood and asked, "Want to get lunch with us?"

"No, I am going to Gina's for a slice of pizza."

"We'll come with you."

"No," Haskell said. "I said I need time to myself."

"At a pizza joint?" asked Ely.

"Gina's is not a pizza joint. Don't call Gina's a pizza joint, you hear?"

Eric and Ely looked at each other. "Hey, why so sweet on Gina's?"

"Mind your own business."
At their father's words, the boys fell to laughing and left.

CHAPTER 40

GATHERING CLOUDS

In lower Manhattan on Mulberry Street, amid the crowded restaurants of Little Italy, stood an array of well-tended narrow, red-brick tenement buildings. The ground floor of one housed Il Puglia, a popular restaurant whose back room was reserved for special meetings and events. Seated there was a group sharing their ideas for the future of their family, their *famiglia*.

"Tell us what Brodsky said, Anthony."

Anthony stood before his cousins in the smoke-filled room. He knew that they were not going to be happy.

"Like you said, I first approached the son. Mostly, he just said, 'Thank you, no thanks.' I approached him three times, and that's all he said. Then I asked to speak to his father, and that's what he said to me: 'Thanks, no thanks.'"

"The Brodsky families are all good people. They did—and I think sincerely—wish us luck with the new plans for the future of our family. They think it's a great idea."

Mario wasn't buying it. "Say what?" he demanded.

"It's a definite no."

The room went still as all eyes turned to Mario. He tilted back, looking down his nose with an expression as if he had never heard the word "no," as if he didn't understand the meaning of it.

"Mario, I was surprised as you are," Anthony said. "However, it is a good step to take the organization straight. New York's a big place. The Brodskys are not the only people in New York that own buildings. There are hundreds of properties around. Let's hire a real estate agent to find some good deals. Just yesterday, I saw a for sale sign on a nice building on Madison Avenue."

Mario was stuck on Brodsky's refusal of his offer. "Those sons of bitches. I like those buildings on Fifth Avenue. What could be better? Do they want more dough?"

"The old man does not want to sell, and he doesn't need partners," Anthony said. "He said that if he wanted to build a tower, which he doesn't, then he could do it himself. His son, who works there, previously worked at an architectural firm that specialized in office building construction. I'm sure they could do it by themselves. They wouldn't need us. They don't need us."

"Fuck him and his fucking do-it-himself. Those Jews want everything for themselves."

Anthony knew he was on dangerous ground. "Mario, Mario, please listen to me. We don't need trouble; we are putting this trouble behind us. It was your brilliant idea to go straight, so no more rough stuff or anything illegal. You must accept someone else's decisions in the legitimate business world. The old days are over."

Everyone laughed. "What the fuck are you assholes laughing at?" Mario spat. Vinnie the Vig spoke up. "Boss, who could be better in the world of business than us? Different business, the American way. Stores, real estate, everyone needs an injection of money. It'll be fun. Let's have fun. Nothing stays the same in America. There are plenty of opportunities for us to take advantage of. There are plenty of people, plenty of stupid people, too, for us to make good deals with. So what if we change; we survive. And anyway, I promised my wife we would."

"Shut the fuck up and let me think," Mario said. "Ditch those fucking cigarettes. They're driving me nuts. Anthony, we need to tell Heshy Levy and his brothers; they're part of this."

CHAPTER 41

OLD WORLD, NEW WORLD, ENTIRE WORLD

E ric summoned the Abraham & Haskell team—including pur-
chasing, production, shipping, and finance—into the conference room. Sandra took notes.

Ely addressed them: "Beginning this week, we will start to plan
and structure our firm to produce as many of our suits and products in Taiwan as soon as possible. We will experience substantial
price savings and become the most competitive in the industry."

Most of the staff assembled there had known Ely since he was a
kid. They were watching him with pride and smiles on their faces.

"All of you will pitch in with your own departments and expertise. Depending on the success, everyone here, including Sandra,
will get significant bonuses—every year, twice a year. You will all
have skin in the game and reap the rewards of your efforts. As
our capacity expands overseas, we will be able to close our factories here. That space will be used for a supplemental coordination
department, which will have translators as well people to evaluate
risk and troubleshoot. In other words, we expect to hire and grow,
not contract out."

Ely continued: "As for the offices, if there is space we don't
need, we'll put it up for lease. Yes, it was convenient, but this property is more valuable as office space than factory space."

"I want to repeat that you will share in our success according to your contribution in this success. I will be moving temporarily to Taipei to open an office, oversee the new operations, and staff it. I will be in touch daily by telephone. I will fly home every four months, or as needed." He turned to Haskell. "I want to thank my father for all he has done, and for entrusting me with the future of the company."

At this, Ely sat down. Eric stood up and applauded. "Thank you, Ely," he said. He turned to everyone else and said, "It is most important, and it is your responsibility, to keep this confidential: we want the field to ourselves. Success in some measure depends on getting ahead of our competition to make the splash we want." He turned to Sandra, who began to distribute the confidentiality agreements. "Everyone here is to sign this pledge of confidentiality. Then you will be attending informational meetings as we continue to lay the groundwork."

Haskell pulled his chair closer to the table and spoke. "You should all be excited. We will be at the forefront. Our company name will be places it never was before. I can imagine sending each of you in turn to Taiwan to see how your departments can improve our operations. We used to be a national company. Now we will be an international conglomerate. How's about that?"

Applause and cheers broke out. Then Haskell waved everyone out but gestured for Eric and Ely to stay.

"I think that went really well!" Ely said exuberantly.

"Poppa, we were Old World, New World, now we're All World!"

Haskell smiled but patted his palms downward. "OK, let's settle down. In all of this, I want you to remember your sister will return, and we need to use her talents. As we move forward, let's keep in mind which responsibilities she can assume when she returns, and consult with her now. Who knows, maybe this will excite her, which would be good, and lure her back sooner."

It was obvious to both Ely and Eric that their father missed Ellen, and they would be well advised to get her to return to the office soon. Plainly, Haskell was as sentimental as he was competitive.

CHAPTER 42

STORM THREATENING

Old habits die hard. Several weeks passed. Mario was furious with the Brodskys. *Thanks, no thanks.* It made his blood boil. *A $5 million offer, and they say, "No thanks."*

In an earlier time, he would send a couple of boys right over to the old man's office and one, two, three, everything would be settled, and a deal made. Now his promise to make the family business legitimate was threatened, and Mario always kept his promises.

The phone ringing startled him "Yeah, what? Who is this?'

"Mario, it's Heshy. I got a message saying you wanted to speak to me. What's up?"

"Heshy, you are a Jew, and I got a problem with some Jewish businesspeople, the Brodskys. Going 'straight' ain't easy, and I need some advice."

"OK, shoot."

"That's just it, I can't."

"You're talking in riddles, Mario. What's on your mind?" Heshy asked cautiously.

"What do you think if I met with the old guy Brodsky face-to-face and told him what I wanted—and made sure he understood my meaning? What do ya think?"

Heshy carefully thought over what his friend and colleague had just said. He didn't want to cross Mario; he was too dangerous and bad tempered. "Here is my advice," he said, "and it would be the opinion of everyone in the organization." He paused; he wanted Mario to hear his recommendation and wanted it to sink in.

"The word has come down from Don Carlo and Meyer and Albert, so listen carefully. These are the orders to every family in the whole country. During these fucking so-called organized crime investigations from that fucking Kefauver committee, lots of shit is going on, and we need less shit. So there will be no mistakes, no noise, nothing. Not a sound. Do you get what I'm saying? We need to use our brains, not our muscles. The word will come when and where we are back in business."

"Are you shitting me? Is this true?" Mario sputtered.

"That's the story."

"Fuck that bullshit! This is *my* territory, and *I* am *capo*, I am the boss. I make my own rules!"

"You're the boss, but I wouldn't fuck with these guys if I were you. You asked for my advice, remember? That's it. Be smart, be careful. Take a vacation, find another building. It ain't worth it."

Mario slammed the phone down, leaving Heshy apprehensive about what was to come.

Later, on Rivington Street, the Levy brothers were about to begin their evening prayers. Heshy waved to command his brothers' attention. "Guys, I just got off the phone with Mario."

"What did he want? Is there a problem?" Tevye asked.

"You know that guy. He's nuts. There's going to be a lot of trouble. We need to get out of here, go to Florida for a month."

"What about our business?" Morris whined.

"Listen to me, moron, it's not important. If we are not here, we will not get into trouble."

"Miami?" Morris asked.

Heshy walked over to the big US map on the wall. He pointed to the tip of the Florida peninsula. "No, not Miami; it's too visible. We are gonna go to Key West and visit our tanta [aunt] Sarah and our cousin Rachel."

CHAPTER 43

ELLEN RETURNS

Ellen came into Eric's office unannounced and plopped down. He ended his business call and asked, "To what do I owe this pleasure?"

"I had to be nearby to sign off on my divorce settlement. Dad says you're working hard. And with Ely in Taipei, and you engaged, he asked me to pitch in. I am ready. Ben is now in school, and I have an afternoon sitter, who will pick him up."

Eric was relieved. With the wedding looming, he could use some help. Grace would be free to assemble the wedding plans. She'd appreciate it.

"When can you start?" Eric asked.

"You tell me."

"Next week."

"Done!" Ellen exclaimed.

"I missed you, kid."

"Don't call me kid, I'm older than you!"

"Duly noted."

Ellen looked at his desk, laden with papers and samples. She looked around and saw the mess of Eric's office, its disarray a clear indication of how much she was needed. She would help take care of whatever matters it represented.

"With Ely gone, I will be the third leg of the tripod with you and Dad," she said. "Look, I can see you're busy. I'll see myself out after I get a hug." Ellen was always a hugger.

The following week, Ellen was back in her old office, which Haskell had given to Ely in the interim. It was as if she had never left. Back then, Ellen had briefed Eric on all business matters, and he was now doing the same with her. As he did, she sketched and scribbled prioritized charts of projects, orders, assignments, and more. Ellen was never without a writing pad.

In no time, the office hummed with newfound vigor, fueled by her energy. More than once, Eric teased her for her intensity, but he admired it.

Haskell was far more relaxed, and everyone seemed happier with her back, including Ellen herself. He understood and realized: *She must have hated to be away for so long. I wouldn't have wanted to go through what she went through.*

CHAPTER 44

TRAGEDY AT GINA'S

Winter came with January winds. One of the benefits of the family garment business was they were always warmly clad. Scotch also helped. Ely was back from Taipei, and finally, Haskell had his three children collaborating with him. Eric's wedding preparations were in full swing. Life was good. Life was . . . very good. Everyone was well and happy. Nobody needed anything. Haskell felt fulfilled.

At noon one day, Haskell asked the kids, "Anyone want pizza? I'm going to Gina's for lunch."

"Since when do you like pizza?" Ellen asked.

"Hannahla, I am an American. That's the custom; ask Eric. He taught me."

"I'm an American, too, so it's Ellen to you, mister, not Hannahla!"

They laughed, but each of the kids declined. Haskell went on alone.

Haskell sat in his regular booth enjoying every bit of the two slices he ordered, plus a 7UP. He and Gina exchanged easy banter and family news. She mentioned that her daughter-in-law, Shirley, was expecting. He offered congratulations and raised his soda in a toast. "To the expectant mother!"

Gina replied, "Which one?"

Confused, Haskell said nothing.

"I am pregnant, Haskell."

Haskell felt like his head was in a bowl, and Gina's voice was floating in from some distant place. Suddenly, he felt a wave of nausea. He put his napkin to his mouth. He had just been smugly reviewing how fine life was, and now he was going to unmake it. Molly would divorce him. He could have to sell the business, give her a building, be uninvited to his son's wedding, his kids would hate him, they wouldn't want to work with him . . . he couldn't stanch the torrent of cascading thoughts of catastrophe.

"Haskell!" Gina put her hand on his.

He stood, unsteady on his feet from the shock. He threw a twenty-dollar bill on the table and stumbled away.

"Haskell!" Gina called after him, but he didn't turn, just raised his hand, and waved. He didn't raise his gaze as he stepped from the curb. A gray Chevy roared down the street. The car smashed into Haskell's body, tossing him in the air. The sound of his bones breaking was audible as his body hit the ground. Gina rushed to his side. A crowd began to form around them as she wailed at the loss of her lover and father of her child. Blood spewed from his mouth.

He was dead. Haskell Brodsky was dead.

Gina clutched her abdomen and stumbled back to the chair he had just left. Losing control, she sobbed, and sobbed, and sobbed.

CHAPTER 45

FLORIDA

The Florida Keys were warm and sunny, only a cloud or two and a welcome breeze. Heshy walked up from a swim in the ocean. He saw his brothers sitting on the open deck, looking down at a newspaper then urgently up to him. "Heshy, Heshy, get over here, at once! Check out the headlines! From the *New York Daily News*!"

"Philanthropist Haskell Brodsky Killed in Hit and Run Accident."

Heshy yanked a chair under himself and sat down. *Mario, that fucking lunatic*, he thought as fear gripped him.

"You were right. It was smart that we are here in Florida. No one would suspect that we were involved."

"Always a moron, Morris! We are involved. Mario called me for advice. We had discussed going into it as partners. But I warned him."

"It wasn't Mario's hit. It was an accident."

"What fucking accident? It was Mario. I wish it were an accident," he said sincerely.

Tevye seemed slightly impressed. "He ordered a hit because a guy wouldn't sell him a building?" Then he said with disgust, "Bad businessman. Mario, I mean."

They all looked at their feet, evaluating how much shit they were in.

CHAPTER 46

FUNERAL AND SHIVA
FOR HASKELL

Haskell's funeral was held at the Park Avenue Synagogue. He would have been thrilled to see it packed with people of different faiths and political positions, the bigwigs he knew, his whole family . . . and Gina.

Among the eulogizers was Stanley Loeb, Haskell's oldest and dearest friend. Not a tall man, he made up for lack of size with impeccable posture and attire. Like Haskell, a man in his midfifties, he was a self-made person.

"Ladies and gentlemen, family, friends, and honored guests." He paused and lifted a handkerchief from his jacket pocket. He gently touched his eye, drying a tear, and continued, "Haskell and I have been friends since he immigrated in 1923. A fairer man, there wasn't. A better husband, there wasn't. A better father, there wasn't. A better grandfather, there wasn't. A harder worker, there wasn't. A better American, there wasn't. A better friend, there surely wasn't. A more generous employer, I have yet to meet. A steady and even increasing supporter of our community, and the wider community . . . Well, he told me he was only beginning!"

Loeb paused, taking a breath as he dabbed his eyes. "We are all robbed, our world depopulated by his loss. From humble beginnings, he lived the American dream. He was beloved!"

Suddenly, Loeb's demeanor changed. "And I say to you, and I howl at the world, my beloved friend Haskell Brodsky's death was no car accident! It was no hit-and-run driver as the newspapers reported; it was murder!"

There was an eruption of murmurs. Protocol had been breached, but he was saying what many in the audience were thinking.

"I will pursue justice for him!" he thundered. "Rest in peace, my friend! You will not be forgotten!"

In a final complete break with protocol, there was a sudden burst of applause. Loeb went to the coffin and kissed it, then sat.

Those who could followed the funeral cortege to the cemetery, where Haskell was buried. Molly barely spoke to anyone, and to her children the frigid temperature seemed a metaphor for a world without their patriarch.

In the late afternoon, guests from every walk of life filled the Brodsky apartment on Central Park West. The mirrors were draped. There was a pitcher for water and a basin to wash one's hands before entering. They signed the condolence book.

Molly and the children sat on crates in the Jewish mourning tradition. Friends and family set out trays prepared in the kitchen and sent by the synagogue's condolence committee. Traditional food and drink and memories were shared. Photographs of the family, especially Haskell, were placed everywhere.

When Stanley Loeb and his wife, Frieda, arrived, the room resounded in cheers of welcome to the hero of the memorial service. He paid his respects to Molly, Ellen, Eric, and Ely, each of whom expressed gratitude for his remarks. He felt particularly sorry for Ben, the one and only grandchild, the apple of his grandfather's eye. Ellen turned to him, tears in her eyes. "The way you said it, was just like Dad would have told it. Thank you."

The gathering met every night for a week of mourning, for shiva. On the sixth night, when the crowd had thinned out, a broad-chested well-dressed man walked over to Eric and extended his hand.

Eric looked into the man's eyes and saw sincerity there.

"I am so sorry for the loss of your father, a terrific guy. He was generous and fair. Might I have a minute? I am a messenger from a friend."

With a glance around the room, Eric beckoned him down the hall into the study and shut the door behind them.

The gentleman spoke first. "You may not know me, but I work for someone who knew your father, and he told me to send his sympathies. My boss remembered your father's generosity to many of our friends when they were just starting out. Many of them were strapped for cash but never left your store without what they needed. Haskell Brodsky made it happen. Here in this envelope is a gratuity to show my boss's gratitude and to compensate for all he has done for us. For this and other matters. We are sincerely sorry. We were shocked and sorry."

Somehow, it wasn't such a surprise. Eric did not bother to ask the man's name, thought it wiser not to, and stood, a man without a father, in his father's stead, ready for whatever came next. He had to take the envelope. He did, but he did not even look at it, never letting his gaze waver from the gentleman's own gaze.

"I am delivering his exact words: whatever help you need, I am here for you."

Eric thought, *This is a dangerous moment. The less I say, the better. I don't want to know what I shouldn't know. How did my father know these people?*

The huge man read his thoughts and answered them. "Kid, your pop was legit. Never took a dime, never paid a dime, not involved. He was always straight. My boss came to his shop early on, and they hit it off. My boss said he would send his friends if they could also negotiate. Negotiating was key. Your dad was great at working things out; he never let anyone leave empty-handed."

The man searched Eric's face before he continued. "Also, your father never asked a question he didn't want to know the answer to. Smart guy. We sent fifty to a hundred Italian immigrants, all friends and family of ours, who came to America like your old man, and your pop gave them all prices they could afford, often wholesale, or even at cost, and on occasion, at no charge. We know about all these deals, all these favors. We keep records. We even know your wholesale prices."

He smiled and gave Eric a small nod. "We have a lot of, say, associated businesses, and they make sure your supplies are delivered and on time. You have a smooth operation, and our friendship is one reason. Just so you know, Abraham & Haskell gets inside-family trucking prices. Ever notice you have zero union problems?"

"Thank you. May I ask a favor of your boss?"

"Speak."

"I have a feeling that the Levy family may have some information about my father's end. Like my dad, I hate to ask a question I shouldn't know the answer to. But I should. Someone who knows more than me could decide if I should know, and what I should know. Right now, I know nothing. Maybe that's best, or it's not. Hard to say. Other people know. So, thank you for coming and paying your respects. We are grateful for your gesture of respect, but we are not taking the money. I return it to you to dispense to other worthy immigrant families, which is what my father would have wanted. Let this charitable gesture be attributed to my father, a fitting memorial."

The gentleman offered no argument, bowing his head and putting the envelope in his inner breast pocket. "This will be known. Your father's good works will be known. And your goodwill, too."

They shook hands again, and the nameless gentleman departed without a look back.

CHAPTER 47

AFTERMATH

The week of deep mourning, prayers, and the constant influx of those coming to pay their respects left everyone exhausted. The business was shuttered for the mourning period. That decision was made jointly by Ellen, Eric, and Ely, and much appreciated by Molly, who needed her children around her. Haskell had been such an influence that now it seemed strange for Molly to be the head of the family. Shiva was not just mourning; it was adjustment.

Throughout the designated mourning week, there was an undercurrent of shock and curiosity about Haskell's demise. Some dared to ask his children, but they knew nothing. Once, Eric recalled Anthony's real estate proposal and wondered if it could be related, but he dismissed it. All he knew was that Haskell had told him that when he spoke to Anthony, he passed on the opportunity. In fact, Anthony and Gina came to pay their respects, and seemed very, very upset at Haskell's passing.

Grace could see that Eric's excitement at planning the wedding had collapsed with his father's death. Taken aback upon learning about the Jewish tradition of a full year's mourning, she took matters into her own hands. Thankfully, with eight weeks before their planned wedding date, no invitations had been sent and the reception hall deposit was still refundable.

"Eric, I have made a hard decision."

"About what, my dear?"

"About us."

"What is the problem?"

"No problem, just an issue to be resolved."

"And that is?"

"I want to be married, and I want to be married more than I want a party or celebration. I want to be married now. A year of mourning is too long to wait. I prefer not to wait any longer. Should I become pregnant, I will feel embarrassed at work. You asked to marry me first; this is my turn to ask you. Are you willing to marry me this week at City Hall?"

He didn't know why he felt a sense of relief.

Grace continued, "If you want, let's do it in your mom's living room, if we can get someone to officiate, but it must be now."

"What do you want?"

"I want to go downtown and say I am married."

On Friday, they both took the day off. They would see everyone at dinner that night at Molly's.

Shabbat dinner started quietly, the empty chair a void no conversation had been able to fill.

Eric asked everyone to sit down and drew a cold bottle of champagne from a duffel bag. He gave everyone a glass, popped the cork, and poured it. "To my wife, Grace! The woman who completes my life. I love you!"

Ellen's eyes locked on Grace's left hand and her wedding band like a laser. "You're married! When?"

"We didn't want to wait any longer," Eric said, "after Poppa's death, and since it's still so soon, we decided to tone it down and did the deed today downtown at City Hall with a justice of the peace."

There was quite a commotion, but Grace didn't care. She had been engaged two years—not considered an unusually long period. Still, it had been an eternity to her.

Ellen looked at her mother, reading her thoughts.

I am going to be a grandmother again! Molly turned to Ellen, then looked at Grace, thinking, *She doesn't look pregnant to me. I wonder why the rush.*

The family's suspicions that Grace might be pregnant were never voiced. However, they were not surprised in midsummer to hear the announcement at a Shabbat dinner at Molly's that a baby was due in January.

Molly was puzzled at the January due date. *So that meant she was not pregnant in March. So why was there a rushed marriage?*

Grace spoke over dessert the night of their announcement: "The loss of our dear Haskell seemed to me to be the defining moment of the family, not a wedding. A wedding might have been overshadowed by the losses we all felt. A wedding was not even allowed by the one-year designated mourning period. I imagine some people would have thought it inappropriate. I am not Jewish; I am also not insensitive."

Grace looked around the table at the people she had grown to love. "When the one-year mourning period is over, we will have a child named after Haskell, and then and only then will we have a celebration. Eric and I already felt married, and we could no longer wait. Since neither family was at City Hall, my father accepted this and understands."

For the remaining months of mourning, Grace had endowed Molly with a new purpose. The new grandchild would go far in making up for their loss.

A week shy of the end of her ninth month, Grace went into labor and delivered her baby after the one-year anniversary of

Haskell's death. Eric, Molly, Ellen, and Ely were at the hospital. The wait seemed interminable. Finally, the doctor emerged, his eyes crinkled behind his mask. He turned to Eric. "Everyone is doing well. Everything is fine. I am glad to see your family is here because you will need extra hands now!"

"Is the baby well?" Ely demanded.

"Yes, I said *everyone* is well."

"Do we have a girl or a boy?" Molly interjected.

"Babies! You have the two-for-one special! You have twin boys. One with blue eyes and one with brown eyes. They are perfect, and Grace is delighted and doing well."

Molly wept like she never had before. She didn't care who saw or heard. When she opened her eyes, the doctor was gone, as was Eric.

Ellen put her arm around her mother's shoulders. "Mom, pull yourself together. This is fantastic! Dad would have been so happy: a two-for-one! We don't pay retail!" At this, Molly laughed.

Eric joined in. "We'll run a two-for one-special."

On the eighth day was the traditional bris. Molly hired a small army to help and invited the world. The blue-eyed boy was named Harrison, after Haskell, and the brown-eyed boy was named Lee, a name Grace chose to honor her grandfather.

As a gift to Grace, Molly hired a baby nurse to help them for six weeks. Watching Grace become sleep deprived prompted Molly to extend the gift until the babies were six months old. The new grandmother's love was made even more manifest than usual. She adored Grace, adored the babies, and visited them every day. She watched as Eric's love for Grace expanded to embrace their sons. The twins saved them all from the depths of their major loss.

It occurred to Eric that his family had never been closer or happier. All this was Grace's work. He recognized her forfeiting a wedding was done for the common good. He respected her insight, her foresight, and inner strength. These riches laid at his feet only sharpened his ardor for her. How true his father's advice: happiness is finding the right woman, and then loving her totally.

The new ratio of responsibilities did not escape Eric's notice. He redoubled his focus at work so his days could be spent efficiently to allow him to leave as early as possible. He could hardly wait to get home after each workday. It was an overwhelming new life, with thoughts of Grace, Harrison, and Lee. This, he finally understood, was how much his parents loved him and his siblings.

Is it possible to be overwhelmed with love, he wondered, with his arm around Grace and his sons in sight? Where did he stop, and they begin? He would do anything for them. He began to realize that his parents had made the same commitment to him, to his sister, and to his brother. He would demonstrate his gratitude to his mother. He was beginning to understand the sacrifices parents make.

CHAPTER 48

CONSEQUENCES

Ely was especially happy; he and Grace had forged a special bond because Taiwan was Ely's responsibility and he considered Grace's presence in their lives a stroke of good fortune.

Their Taiwan factory was producing smoothly. The results were as expected: costs decreased, and profits increased. The firm was able to offer prices slightly lower than their competitors. Still, they had room for negotiating. The Abraham & Haskell hallmark was simple: *quality, speed, reliability, value.* Their office writing pads had those words along the top. Their stationery had it at the bottom. The business cards had it on the back. That philosophy encompassed their entire operation. To meet their own standards, there was no room for slack. Business flourished; their Canadian market expanded dramatically. How sad that Haskell did not live to see it. The void left by Haskell was filled by others at the office. Life, indeed, went on.

• • •

Spring was on the horizon when an unexpected call came in. The caller was not identified; his deep voice carried an Italian accent. "Eric, my name is Carlo. I was close to your father, but at a distance. I am sorry I was unable to personally pay my respects to your father, but I sent one of my associates, Rico. He said you spoke to him privately. You asked a favor. I'm the one who does the favors." Carlo stopped to let the words sink in before he continued.

"Oh, and thank you for the cordial welcome you gave him. Not always the case in our family business; much appreciated. We will remember that."

Eric caught on immediately. He knew this day might come. Now his heart was racing. He spoke with care: "Your condolences were noted. My family appreciates the concern of your family. As family men, let's talk."

"Eric Brodsky, your father was a very generous man to my family and friends. May he rest in peace. Like you, we were not happy with what, uh, transpired. We were curious, too. Me, I am not happy when my curiosity is not satisfied."

Eric's heartbeat pounded in his ears. *I am in over my head; this is not something I want to get involved with!*

The man continued, "Eventually, we will speak more when there is more to say. For now, you are not alone, but our conversations are confidential, just between us. There, that's it." With that, the caller hung up.

CHAPTER 49

SORTING IT OUT

Life did not stop for love or children. Business demanded Eric's attention equally. There was trouble. He was caught on the horns of a dilemma. Carlo, whom he came to find out was also known as Don Carlo, needed an answer soon. Did he want who-ever had killed his father to be whacked? Would he, Eric, authorize punishment or violence against another human being? He knew "Thou shalt not kill." He surprised himself when he had asked Don Carlo for a week to think it through.

He told no one how he suspected that Mario ordered his father's death for refusing to sell his building or go into business with him. His own hate was not a permission slip. This was not a cure. This was open-ended; what if Mario's family came back to his family? Mario had adult children and a sphere of criminals sur-rounding him. Eric had to protect everyone in the Brodsky family. He now had two children and his wife. This was not a game. The risk exceeded emotions.

His response to Carlo was, "You do whatever your needs may be. For my part, I am staying out of it." Keeping the Brodsky fam-ily safe was his first priority. They were all in too deep. It was a losing proposition to join Don Carlo's anger.

Eric mulled over how much Anthony knew, including his possible involvement; both were unknown. *What do I know about*

Anthony's history? Or Anthony's deceased father, a man never mentioned? he wondered. *Was Gina's Pizza a front, not just a restaurant? Nothing is as it seems, nor is it otherwise,* his father's words replayed on a loop in his brain. Anthony married into the Levys—and three Levy brothers killed Uncle Abe. His father and his uncle—both murdered by the mob. Would he be next? *Did Anthony connect Haskell and Abe? Why did his father insist on going to Gina's that fateful day? Had someone at Gina's tipped off Mario?*

Yet he saw Anthony every workday, and Anthony was oblivious to his suspicions. *He seems honest, dependable. How could I question Anthony's role or connections?* But finally, he realized the sight of Anthony riled him. He knew it was time for a confrontation. He no longer cared if Anthony added value to the company; no one was indispensable.

He invited Anthony to have lunch with him at a small diner on Thirty-Fourth Street, a quiet spot. He was in no mood to play cat-and-mouse.

"I know the whole story, Anthony," he started. "You bragged about your position here and how prosperous the business was . . . is. You blabbed about our owning buildings. Your boasting, either intentionally or unintentionally, brought unwanted attention and enmeshed my family in mob business. You were the intermediary; you are the cancer. Were you going to get a piece of our buildings, and never tell us? You were a traitor to my family." Eric felt his rage build.

"We put the clothes on your back, we hired you, we danced at your wedding, we celebrated when your wife was expecting, and we forgave your wife's relatives. You dragged me into this by approaching me. What part did you play in Mario's revenge? You're a sellout! You had my father killed because that might make me buckle under to the takeover!"

Very quietly, very steadily, Anthony asked, "Who told you this bullshit story?"

"Don Carlo."

"Oh . . . How did he learn all this?"

"He knows everything. He and my father went back a long time. You stepped in shit for this. You are now on his shit list, too. You don't piss without him knowing it."

Anthony reached into his back pocket and placed both hands palms down on the table. He had a card in one hand, a small card he turned over to show it to Eric. On it was a picture of a saint. Anthony tapped its edge against the table. "You know, in all the years we have known each other, you have never cared to find out what I believe. This is my patron saint. I am named for St. Anthony. My mother lost two children by miscarriage before me, and named me in honor of St. Anthony, the patron saint of lost things, because I was not lost. My mother gave me this card after my Nonna passed; it was hers. It stood on her night table, and she looked at it when she said her rosary. I swear on St. Anthony and Nonna's grave that I urged just the opposite: I communicated that the answer was, 'Thanks, but no thanks.' I tried to calm Mario; I told him there are real estate agents whose whole job it is to find us property, that there were other opportunities. I never spoke to him or saw him after that. I swear it."

"Swear it on your wife and children."

"I swear it on my wife and children."

"So, what is your defense?"

"I am a fool. It was a mistake to agree when Mario asked me for the favor of an introduction or to be a messenger to Haskell. I thought, *Don't do this, don't do this.* But I didn't think it through. Please forgive me."

"Talk is cheap, Anthony, if I even believe you. You seem comfortable playing with other people's lives. So, I put Mario's life in your hands; since you helped set all this in motion, it's only fitting. Does Mario live, or does Mario die? He's your relative."

"Of course, you can't have him killed! Are you crazy, too, now? For God's sake, Eric, you need to understand these guys are never through. Nothing ends. Are you stepping in? With what? You're a civilian! You're considering whether to ally yourself with Carlo when your father wouldn't ally himself with Mario? Have you become what your father rejected? You're going to be associated with Carlo now? You think that's healthy?"

"Fuck you." Eric said, barely holding back his rage.

"I deserve that. But please, sit tight. Give me overnight. I want to see what, if anything, we can find out from Shirley's relatives in the investment business."

"Come on. You expect me to believe that you haven't already asked around?"

"I did. They were visiting relatives in Florida when your father died."

"Oh, you think because they were in Florida, they knew nothing before or after?" Eric sneered.

"Well, it's been over a year. It can wait another night. Let me find out what I can."

"Let me know by tomorrow morning. Meet me here at the diner at eight with the answers. Get it right."

The next day, Eric was ten minutes early. He had finished his coffee when Anthony slid into the booth.

"You got an answer for me?"

Anthony sat down, ordered coffee black. He added some sugar, took a sip, and began. "Mario knew the rules. The big bosses sent down instructions: no one does anything—nothing, zero. That's it.

Everyone is on high alert because of the mob hearings in Congress. Their final order was to *lay low*. Stupidly, Mario defied them, taking the issue with your father into his own hands. His stupidity brought more heat to all the families. All the families, Eric.

"For that alone, for the honor of all the families and then for defying them, they gave the order to knock off Mario. Make him disappear. But he bought his life back and made peace by giving up most of his territory and his goons. The bosses were revolted that he risked so much when—I don't mean to insult you—there were a million other buildings and Mario should have taken, 'Thanks, no thanks' for an answer in these circumstances and moved on.

"Your family is on a do-not-touch list now. But if you bring heat, then I don't know. It was all Mario; you don't have to go looking for other villains. I say, leave it alone. All the families turned away from Mario. No one has his back, and if he finds himself in another pickle, no one will lift a finger to help him. I think he's on thin ice now, and now you need to stop asking questions."

"Anthony," Eric said, feeling older than his years, "I must let you go. You can no longer work for our company. I can't be part of any of this; I don't want to look at you and remember your pitch to sell our buildings that started all this. And if something happens to Mario, at some point, the police could get involved, and I want to be as far away from that as possible. If Mario gets hurt, I am only one step away from him, Carlo, and you. That is too close."

Eric leaned in toward Anthony. "So, listen to me, my friend. You can stay here up to a month; I want you to put it out that you are looking for something else and make it your idea. I want you to tell that version to everyone. Tell them, 'I left because it was time to try something new.' In return, I will give you a sterling job recommendation, and we will not refer to this again should our paths cross. My family business was built on toil, nothing else. I won't have it soiled. Go now, and I'll take care of the check here and get back to the office, where we will act like nothing else is going on. I want this sordid business buried with my dad. I want my business to be only about business from here out. Keep your mouth shut and I will keep mine shut, too."

Anthony got up slowly, looking at Eric in disbelief as his eyes welled up and a tear or two escaped. He started to speak, but then closed his mouth. He didn't blame Eric; he blamed Mario. No harm that might come to Mario should be traceable to the Brodskys.

It was a toss-up which of them felt worse.

CHAPTER 50

FALLOUT

Mario felt a crush in his heart when the telephone rang. He let it ring. He made no effort to answer. It rang again. He did not answer. A rapid stress-free moment passed until it rang once again. His only move was for the glass of whiskey on the kitchen table. It did not stop him from smelling trouble. He moved away from the kitchen window, not wanting to be an easy target. Mario thought, *When Don Alberto wants to meet with someone, it's not an invitation, it's an order.* He knew he was about to find out the price of his defiance.

Mario knew himself well enough that by nature, he was bullish. This was his calling, and his talent, one of the few he had. He regarded Borough Park, Brooklyn, as *his* personal neighborhood. He'd perfected his tough-guy persona, reveled in the dread he inspired, felt invigorated by the forced deference as passing men tipped their hats, young women smiled. Mario had made himself known to all in the neighborhood. As he made his rounds or strolled the streets, greeted by all, he'd think, *Santa Claus has nothing on me!*

But today was different. He sat isolated at his linoleum kitchen table. He imagined a bowl of fear in front of him. He knew and remembered it was he whom everyone feared.

At last the telephone stopped ringing. Suddenly, he heard a knock at the door. He hesitated. The knocking didn't stop.

"Mario, Mario, are you OK? Answer the door! It's me, Heshy."

Relieved, Mario opened the door, but there was another man there with Heshy. Heshy pushed his way in; the other man followed.

Heshy spoke first. "What's happened to you, my friend? You've disappeared?"

"Who's this fucking guy with you?"

"Calm down. He's one of our people. Ziggy, please say hello to Mr. Tracci. He's the boss here."

Ziggy grunted in what was meant to be a friendly tone. Mario nodded in return.

"What's wrong, Mario? You've gone missing. It's been noticed."

"Albert says he wants to see me," Mario answered.

"So, why are you acting scared? You are in charge here. Did you skim from the take?"

"I'm not scared, and I did not skim," Mario said faintly.

"Are you selling drugs without permission from the syndicate?"

"Never."

"Well, all the entitlements to the bosses going on time?"

"Without fail, every cent. I send Fat Vinnie with the cash every week," Mario replied.

"Could Fatso be putting his hand in the drawer?"

"Who knows? It's possible; anything's possible. But he's the one guy I trust."

"You didn't do anything with this Brodsky guy, right?" Heshy paused. "I mean, you knew not to."

Mario hesitated, too, for the millisecond that told Heshy what he didn't want to know but needed to.

"I swear on my mother's grave, I was not on that hit," Mario said.

Heshy was much smarter than Mario, though he would never let on. *Mario gave it away*, he thought, *with one word: hit. Not accident. Hit. Whatta schmuck. I told him to take a vacation. He did this to himself. And for what?*

Heshy's voice was pleasant. "So, you have nothing to worry about. There's a reorganization, or a new position for you. Could be he wants you to manage a special favor. Anyway, you gotta see him." Ziggy sat, impassive, his expression giving nothing away.

Heshy continued, "Mario, my friend, today I got a call from Albert's number two. Because you and I are friends, he reached out to ask me and Ziggy to bring you out to his Great Neck palace. Seen his mansion? Amazing. Get your coat."

Heshy smiled, keeping his voice steady and assured. Mario wanted to believe he wasn't being set up, but he didn't have a choice now. He looked around his kitchen and reluctantly got his coat. He touched the pocket and felt his gun. Ziggy opened the door, and they all left.

As they approached Heshy's black Lincoln town car, Mario was surprised to see Morris Levy, Heshy's brother, in the driver's street. He stopped walking. For the last time, he was still boss.

Mario summoned his old self. "Heshy, Ziggy, come with me to the back of the car. This is my turf. I shouldn't need protection here, but these days, the world's upside down."

He rapped on the driver's window, and Morris rolled it down. "Come, step out, my friend," Mario said to Morris.

The three visitors knew what was about to happen. They allowed Mario to frisk them: no guns, no axes, knives, liquids— clean. Mario, in turn, allowed himself to feel a slight relief.

Heshy stood squarely in front of him. "We are not armed; we are here on a favor to you and Mr. A. Please believe me, Mario, you're gonna be safe with us. This meeting could be the best thing for you. Like you said, you paid up every month, no drugs, no skimming, nothing bad. It's a walk in the park."

Ziggy went around the car to get into the back seat, on the passenger's side. Heshy opened the front passenger door and motioned for Mario to get in.

"Relax," Heshy ordered. "Morris, drive carefully. I want Mario to feel comfortable." Mario saw the three men were smiling.

They sped along the Brooklyn-Queens Expressway onto the Belt Parkway. There was little traffic this late Sunday afternoon.

"Why did Albert call you?" Mario asked Heshy. "He knows everyone's number."

"Seems you don't always answer. So, I got tapped. Simple."

When they had driven an hour and were about twenty minutes from Mr. A.'s mansion, Mario thought Morris kept looking into the rearview mirror.

"Why do you keep looking out the rearview?" Mario asked anxiously.

"Cops. It's a habit. Always looking for police."

They pulled off the main highway at exit 33. "Shit. Need gas," Morris said. He pulled into what looked to Mario liked a closed gas station, but there was another car at the pumps. In one moment, Mario recognized the other car. It was the gray Chevy—with the same guys he'd hired for the Brodsky hit. It was a setup.

"You are fucking son of a bitch Jew bastard! Let me out of this fucking car!" The door was locked. Suddenly it wasn't. Mario, screaming, was pulled out and into the open back seat of the Chevy. A dark cloth reeking of chloroform crushed across his face, smothering him unconscious. The car took off, gravel spraying behind its wheels.

Within a mile, Mario was pushed out. His neck snapped as his head struck the pavement at eighty miles an hour.

The Chevy's speed dropped to thirty-five miles per hour at exit 34 on the Sunrise Highway toward Great Neck.

Ziggy checked his watch, made a thumbs-up. He turned to Heshy and Morris. "Like clockwork," he said.

They pulled up to Mr. A.'s mansion and were buzzed past the driveway gate. Morris blinked his headlights three times in the direction of the front door as he had been instructed, signaling a successful mission. There stood Mr. A., the big boss, waving them to come in.

There were no introductions. They stopped in the foyer, where an envelope sat on a table on a silver platter. Alberto picked it up and handed it to Heshy. "Thank you," was all he said to his visitors.

"No, thank you. We were honored to be of help. No money, please, you will insult us."

Alberto smiled and replied, "Someday, you may need a favor; please don't hesitate to reach out and call me."

The meeting was over. Alberto extended his hand, and they all shook. Mr. A.'s guard opened the door, and they left the mansion. It took all of five minutes, this meeting. They were back inside their car before the engine had cooled.

Morris turned to Heshy. "We should have taken the money."

"Morris, be smart," Heshy answered. "Which is better: Cash today, or a genie's wish granted tomorrow? Money comes and goes, but a favor like this is money in the bank—or better. Who knows? Someday, it might save your life."

CHAPTER 51

THE MORNING AFTER

Eric was at his desk early, even before Sandra arrived. The telephone rang, and he answered it to hear an unfamiliar voice.

"Mr. Brodsky?"

"Yes?"

"You do not know me, but a mutual friend told me to contact you and advise that Mario Tracci died in a car accident yesterday." *Click.* The line went dead. Eric held the receiver in his hand and stared at it like it was alive.

He didn't know how long he sat motionless, his face pale. Sandra arrived and looked in to see Eric turn away, staring out the windows at the skyline.

"Are you OK?" she asked.

He looked at Sandra like he was about to cry. "I don't know, I don't know."

"Tell me about it," she inquired gently.

One step away, he thought. *I am only a step away from being connected to this disaster. Thank God Anthony left.* "A friend died. Shocked and surprised, that's all. I just need to digest it. Sandra, please leave me and shut the door. I'll be out soon. I just need a few minutes to myself."

CHAPTER 52

A BUSINESS PROPOSAL

March 1957. The phone startled Eric out of a deep sleep. "Hello, hello, who is this?"

"Eric, it's Ely."

"Ely, you know it's three in the morning. Are you all right? What's happening? Why are calling me at this hour?"

"I'm fine. Big business news; I couldn't wait to tell you. Our suit factory partners in Taipei are in the mood for acquisitions."

"Go on, quickly, please."

"They want us to consider going into joint ventures with them or selling them our company."

"Give me a minute." He looked over at Grace, who was sleeping peacefully. He slipped out of bed, pulled the cord into the bathroom, and shut the door. "Details, Ely."

"Mr. Hi Beau from the Ying Shen factory asked me if my partners would consider a merger or a total buyout, all cash."

"When are you supposed to come back? Something like this is not going to get done on the telephone."

"I can come home anytime you say, or I can stay as long as needed."

Eric heard something different in his brother's voice. An extra spark, more than excitement about a business deal.

"Ely?" he questioned. "You got a girlfriend in Taipei?"

"And how!" Ely said enthusiastically.

"Well, it's too late, er, too early here to get into that. What's his number? I'm not saying we are even interested, but what are we talking about?"

There was interference on the line, and it went dead. After five minutes, Eric went back to bed. He didn't have to think about this. He wasn't interested in selling his family business.

Ely called again at noon. It was midnight Asia time. After conferring with Ellen, Eric suggested Ely come home.

Two days later, Ely's plane landed in New York at eight in the morning. He cleared customs and took a cab directly to the office with his luggage.

Ely had spent the overnight flight working to calculate the worth of Abraham & Haskell for a sale, or the terms for an advantageous merger. He arrived with his tie loosened, shirt wrinkled, and smiling ear to ear.

Ellen greeted him with, "You reek! Why didn't you go home and shower first?"

Ely laughed. "Thanks, but I've already got a mom."

In the conference room, a tray of orange juice, black coffee, and Ely's favorite danish had been laid on the credenza. Ely spoke into the intercom: "Thanks, Sandra. Your thoughtfulness makes me feel at home again."

"Clearly, you had an extraordinary trip in Asia," Ellen said. "Tell us everything, especially pertaining to Mr. Hi Beau."

Ely was a young man in a hurry. "Mr. Hi Beau is the owner of the Ying Shen factory in Taipei. He graduated from the University of Chicago, economics major, minor in business administration. Got his master's from National Taipei University in mechanical engineering. He believes our companies, together, can dominate the men's, women's, and children's global apparel market. His vision is in the billions."

Ely waited, watching the faces of Eric and Ellen. "His company has spared no expense constructing the most modern clothing factories in Taipei and most of Asia, which is saying a lot. He has an automation expert and has added a top-notch finishing department, which is why we've been happy with them. And they are very satisfied with us. We pay our invoices on time. Our orders represent serious volume for them, which has made them ambitious."

"Sounds interesting. What is his proposal?" Ellen had reviewed proposals from many companies eager to share the Brodsky success. As always, she reserved her opinion before responding.

"He offered to buy us out or partner with us. He is a marketing genius. Their label is ubiquitous in Asia. His family is wealthy. They have a small shipping line and are looking for a Western foothold." Ely's excitement was palpable. "Hi Beau envisions using our collaboration to become a top-tier international supplier. He says they have the resources to reach every retailer on the globe."

In spite of his reservations, Eric warmed to the possibilities Ely proposed. "To think of all the suits and coats Poppa made and sold from this very building . . . I was with him. He loved it. I wish he were here with us today. He should be here to experience how things have changed and will continue to change."

"Hey, wait a minute," Ely said. "I don't understand. You're saying Dad loved retail? I thought his first love was manufacturing. Why was that?"

"Retail gave him cash in hand. No terms, no waiting for payment. No calling retailers who owed money. For him, it was simple and easy. But I think he would be interested in expanding; that's been the nature of the business from the start."

Ely looked hopeful.

"I like Mr. Hi Beau's ideas enough to continue listening," Eric said. "Ellen?"

Ellen had been paying close attention. "Poppa always said, 'No harm in talking.' Mr. Hi Beau needs to be willing to come here and meet in person, if we move into serious discussions."

"So, Eric, Ellen, if you approve, I am going to ask him to put his proposals in writing," Ely said. "If we are still interested after that, let's get him here."

"Ely," Ellen said, "I am so proud of you. This could be something huge. Thank you for the tireless work you have put into our future. An opportunity to open manufacturing in Taiwan will give us an enormous asset. Obviously, with Ben being so young and the twins only toddlers, Eric and I need you to fill the slot as our international wingman. I have the feeling this may be how you make your mark in the family business."

"You're right, Ellen," Eric said. "Ely, this is, and should be, your baby, your project. Havrohm, Moishe, Solomon, Haskell . . . and now, Ely!"

Ely's face broke into a huge boyish grin.

Eric cleared his throat. "Is this the time to start considering new titles? We're partners, but do we want, do we need corporate titles?"

"Is 'Queen' a title?" joked Ellen.

"Well, Ellen has the most years in. So shouldn't she be president?" Ely asked.

Ellen laughed. "No, no, that doesn't sit well with me. Don't you remember Dad calling me 'She-who-will-not-be-denied'? I don't need that anymore."

"How about we are all vice presidents?" Ely said.

"We need a president," Eric said.

"We could draw straws," Ellen suggested.

Ellen spoke up, this time in a serious voice. "I don't want either of you to have opportunities I don't; it's not fair. I propose we have rotating two-year terms as president. I nicknamed us the tripod out of recognition that we are all necessary and equal. So, I hereby nominate myself to be first because of seniority, then Eric, then you, Ely. It just so happens to be chronological, so it's logical and fair. And it will give Ely a bit more time to build on this success."

Ely turned to his sister and his brother. "I second the nomination of Ellen to be president for the first two-year term, starting today. You know, I hardly imagined this might be an opportunity for me in the company. I like the way this can work out for all of us."

Ely looked at his brother. "Eric, what do you think?"

Eric turned to his sister. "Madam President, what is your pleasure?"

"Focus on your responsibilities. Do not go off course. Report to me every morning. Tell me the truth, good and bad. Help me be a successful president. We are adjourned."

Ellen stood, and her brothers mock-bowed, and they all burst out laughing.

CHAPTER 53

THE PROTÉGÉ

A year after Haskell's death, Eric got a surprise call from Anthony. "Eric, are you free for lunch today or any day this week?"

"Why?"

"For old times' sake."

"Nothing funny?"

"That's history. This is friendship. I want to see you. I miss our friendship."

They settled on meeting at a quiet Irish bar where they would not be seen by anyone they knew.

Anthony was all small talk, but Eric was wary. "Enough small talk. What is this really about?"

"Eric, I want you to know that my family was crushed by your father's death. Shirley and I definitively broke off with the Levy brothers. My close relatives have disassociated themselves with the Tracci family branch. My mom needed me to come help, so I joined her in the Gina's Pizza business. We have left the dark history behind."

Anthony watched Eric's face. "I never had a father," Anthony said. "Haskell was like a father to me."

"That's good." The truth was, he didn't care anymore. He never thought of Anthony, never went to Gina's. Eric missed his father. He wondered if there was another point to this lunch. Was Anthony feeling him out for something?

Anthony continued. "But that's a digression—an important one. I don't want to change the course of our conversation. I watched Mom work hard each day. One day I got an idea from a restaurant in Chinatown. Do you remember that Mom had one menu, a blackboard that hung from the ceiling?"

"All right, Anthony. So, tell me, what did you come up with? A regular printed menu?" Eric tried to appear interested.

"No, better, but that's a good guess. I made paper menus to give to everyone to take home. They call, we cook, we bag it, then they pick up the food. Found money. Business doubled. We hired delivery boys with bikes; they are all hard workers. We pay for each delivery, and they keep their tips. We enlarged the oven and hired another cook. This past year was our best. We opened another restaurant in the Brownsville section of Brooklyn. It is going gangbusters. A customer who is a banker got us lines of credit and has introduced us to his investment club."

Eric looked away, unable to hide his reaction.

"Don't worry, it's legit!" Anthony said. "An attorney is giving us money to open a restaurant in Hell's Kitchen, midtown, west side. If that goes well, the investment club will recommend us to their members, and we plan to offer each of them an opportunity to open another restaurant."

Anthony's details melted into the memory of how his father loved the cash business.

"Now, you ask, who's the boss? Me! I am the new family boss!" Anthony said. He puffed his chest out. "I owe this all to your father, who taught me everything."

For the first time in years, Eric laughed with his old friend. This could be a new beginning. They were not in an adversarial position anymore. For the rest of their lunch, they reverted to enjoying each other's company once again.

Eric left thinking how sad it was that Poppa did not live long enough to celebrate his protégé's accomplishments. *I know Poppa would have been so happy with Gina's success. He was always fond of Anthony and Gina.*

As Eric watched Anthony walk away, he saw that his friend looked like a burden had been lifted. He wondered if, with this reconciliation, he had forgiven Anthony.

CHAPTER 54

EAST MEETS WEST

The written proposals from Hi Beau supported moving forward. Within a month, the company was ready to meet with their Taipei counterparts.

Mr. Hi Beau, the *laoban,* the big boss of his giant conglomerate, arrived, accompanied by his wife, known as his *tai tai,* and his son, Joseph Beau, acting as his *sha laoban*, or underboss. They landed in New York the first Monday in May 1957.

The Hi family had insisted on making their own arrangements for lodgings and chose to stay at the Waldorf Astoria on Park Avenue. They politely refused Ely's offer to greet them at the airport and bring them into the city. Since both the elder and younger Hi had been in and out of the United States on other occasions, Ely knew they were comfortable on their own managing their planning and understood they would not want to meet until they had recovered from the long flight.

Ely had filled Eric and Ellen in on their guests beforehand: Ely knew their personalities, their proclivities, and their dislikes. He knew their customs and manners. He had done his homework.

Joseph Beau followed in his father's footsteps and had attended the University of Chicago, where he also majored in economics. His mother had met her husband at the National Taipei University when she was getting her master's in mathematics while he pursued his master's in engineering.

Madam Hi was excited to finally see New York City: the Empire State Building, the Metropolitan Museum, and most important for her, the Statue of Liberty. Her tour of the city would have to wait, though—business first. The Hi family needed to verify that the Abraham & Haskell Company was what they needed.

Generations of the Hi family had been believers in the power of education to work in tandem with close family ties. They had begun as silk merchants, then as producers of silks and other fabrics. Soon, they moved into manufacturing clothing. As that grew, they invested in one ship, then another, then another. Now their three ships sailed on a regular schedule to many Asian destinations. Like the Brodskys, as they grew, they acquired real estate and flourished.

Hi Beau and his son arrived at the offices of A&H promptly at 10:00 a.m. Sandra greeted them in Mandarin. Hi Beau and his son both smiled.

"Mr. Brodsky, his brother, and his sister are expecting you," she told them.

Sandra clicked on her intercom and said, "Our guests have arrived."

In an instant, Ely was at the door to welcome Hi Beau and Joseph. Ellen and Eric saw how their brother welcomed the Hi Beau family. Ely was greeted in return with genuine affection.

Both father and son bowed respectfully, and presented their business cards to Eric, holding them with both hands. Eric accepted them with a slight bow as he read the cards. He offered his own held in the fingertips of both hands, with its newly printed Chinese translations as Ely had suggested.

They moved into Eric's office. The senior Hi Beau took a fleeting look around the room, surprised by photos, books, and many pieces of art covering the walls. He experienced a feeling of comfort as a deep breath crossed his chest. He turned to his son and said in Mandarin, "Very nice office, very American." His son responded with a grin, recognizing his father's sense of humor.

Sandra entered the office, holding a tray with an assortment of drinks.

"Gentlemen," Hi Beau began, "you have a brave, hardworking colleague. Who, with patience and extraordinary skills, has taught us how to improve our production and the quality of our products. We are grateful to you."

"Mr. Hi Beau," Ely said, "we are a family business. Ellen is our sister and a principal in our company. We try to strengthen our vision and our direction with all the genetic potency given to us by our parents and grandparents and their parents before them. Strange enough, it works; not only for us, but it will work for the fourth generation as well."

Hi Beau stood by his chair. "In our first moments, meeting you and your brother and sister, watching how you respect each other—it demonstrates consideration, flexibility, and the intelligence to deduce at once that the next generation is an important part of your plans with your family and your company." Hi Beau sipped some water and continued, "We, too, are a similar family enterprise. I am in the second generation, and my son, Joseph, at my side, is our third generation."

Eric sat in silence, nodded slightly in Ely's direction. They shared the same thought: *this guy is very smart; it's time to just listen and learn.*

"Mr. Hi Beau, please continue," Ely said. All eyes turned to Hi Beau. With his fluent English, this very elegant man began. He spoke with much care, explaining his global plans to merge both companies as a single conglomerate. The plan was to meld both groups to cover the entire globe. His scope was to market their merchandise to both wholesalers and consumers. He said technology was the future of worldwide marketing, and the first step in worldwide sales. "We want your family business to join our vision of the future," he said. "It is ours for the taking."

Silence filled the room. Mr. Hi Beau was brilliant in his presentation. Everyone was impressed.

Eric stood and shook Hi Beau's hand. "Let's have lunch with further discussions," he said. "Then we would like to retire to our offices with our family to discuss your proposal privately and return to you with questions, ideas, and proposals. Is tomorrow morning at breakfast good for you?"

The room suddenly got quiet. Everyone was surprised. There was no response. Hi Beau and his son left.

Ellen, Eric, and Ely sat silently in their showroom. No one spoke.

Ellen looked straight into Eric's face. Her voice was quiet. "I have always admired you, your sales skills, and in particular your business talents. This morning you failed on every level, not to mention, you were rude to these people who traveled from the other side of the globe to meet with us." Ely lit up a cigarette. He puffed out a little smoke and began. "Ellen is right. I have never seen you so rude. What's going on?"

No one spoke, and finally Eric stood up. "I have worked my entire life in Poppa's footsteps. I have not a clue what technology he is talking about or what international marketing is about."

Elen responded, "This is the beginning of a new world in marketing and sales. A new time and generation for manufacturing. Which is why we are in Asia before any of our competitors. Do you know what Poppa would have said to Hi Beau? He would have said, 'Thank you for coming to visit us. You made a long trip to offer us this opportunity, and there is no harm in talking. America is a new world to us. And I have always valued the opportunity America offers us. Now we are being offered an opportunity to take our business around the globe.' Were he still alive, he would have thanked Hi Beau for his input then turned to us and said, 'There is no harm in talking.'"

Eric and Ely turned to each other. There was no anger on their faces. Instead, they both smiled and nodded in agreement. "Ellen, you are exactly like our father," Ely said.

"OK," interrupted Eric, "talk now, or later after lunch?"

"Let's talk now!" they said in one voice.

The conversation covered several issues.

Ely turned and began, "I understand your position perfectly. Here are my thoughts. I want to do it with Hi Beau. I want to work in Asia. I love it there. I suggest we sell our company to our new friends in China. We take the proceeds and distribute them to our partners and our valued employees. And though we sell, no one in our company will lose their jobs. Including you both."

Ely touched Eric's knee. "Ellen is right, let's do it." The brothers began to laugh.

"What are you guys laughing at?" Ellen asked.

Eric turned to Ellen. "We are laughing because you sound and think just like Poppa."

All three discussed it and produced a sales figure of $35 million.

CHAPTER 55

THE SECRET LIFE OF POPPA HASKELL

Eric and Anthony continued to meet regularly over the years, old friends enjoying their shared memories of Haskell's passion for his business and his devotion to his family.

On this day, they quieted, enjoying the miso soup in front of them, steaming, hot, and clear.

"It's been twenty years since you took over your mother's restaurant," Eric said. "Look how far you've come. Our history of the past couple of decades is nowhere as exciting as yours has been. The A & H business has grown on a slow, but steady path. My father's decision to close production in the States turned out to be brilliant. We prospered; we live well. Our children are off to college now and are mostly grown. I love my kids, but it's strange that I am experiencing a special connection to my nephew, Ben, Ellen's son. He's twenty-six now and reminds me so much of my father."

"How do you mean?" Anthony had met Ben, and often reflected on his own early years working for Haskell.

"Well to begin with, he looks exactly like his grandfather, except taller. He works hard and minds his own business. Never interfering at any level in anyone's life or concerns. He met a lovely Chinese woman when he managed our investment in Asia. They married and had a son and twin daughters."

A strange look came over Anthony's face. Eric could not decipher it. Something twisted in his gut. He knew to pay attention to this as an important signal; he knew it as that sixth sense that sends a warning sign. He knew from experience not to brush off that familiar feeling.

Eric turned away and called to their waiter. "Please bring me a double espresso," he said. "You want to join me, Anthony?"

"No, thanks, I'm fine." The quiet restaurant calmed both men, a brief respite from their busy days.

"Anthony, I am so pleased we have been meeting all these years. Thank you. It's good for both of us. Now, I have a question," Eric said. "I want the absolute truth, no matter what. Can you agree?"

"I have never told you anything that was not the truth. But it's an unfair request, asking me to agree to something before I know what I am promising."

Both men sat in silence. Neither wanted to break the spell of goodwill and friendship that had sustained them over the years.

"I saw an expression on your face, in your eyes, one that I had never seen before, even with all we have been through," Eric said. He could not hold back. He took a deep sip of espresso and said, "We were talking about Ben. Do you know something I don't know?"

"No, I have no information about Ben that is particularly important," Anthony said. "What I do know is that your dad was proud of his children and especially filled with pride about Ben. But he always worried about this grandson. He was concerned that the boy might sink into the dishonest habits of his father. Poppa Haskell was always thinking, constantly. He was troubled about the traits that could pass from Marvin to Ben."

It was late afternoon; most of the diners were gone. The waiters were cleaning up, the only sounds the hum of the air conditioners and the snap of fresh linens unfurled over the tables for the dinner hour.

Eric sat back in his chair. "Anthony, I want to hear everything. Leave nothing out. I promise you will not hurt my feelings, and I will appreciate your honesty and integrity. Your mother is, how old? I am guessing, early sixties? My father has passed twenty years or more. Tell me everything you know."

CHAPTER 56

REVELATIONS

Anthony looked at his watch and sipped his coffee. He looked up at the server, pointed to his cup and nodded. She understood.

Anthony shut his eyes for a moment and made a decision, its fleeting thought sweeping through his mind. He exhaled, and he began.

"Your father came to lunch very often, every day. But he was smart; he used to come to Gina's at about one thirty in the afternoon. It was less busy at that time."

Eric stared into his friend's eyes. He had a glimmer of a thought of what might be coming. Anthony went on.

"Each time he came for lunch, my mom would sit with him. They would talk for an hour or more. She would get up and give him another can of 7UP. Until one day I heard her say, 'Haskell, this drink is not good for you. Let me make you a cup of tea.'"

Eric could not believe what he was hearing. He knew then and there that Gina was in love with his father. Those words, that simple statement, was exactly what his mom would say to his father when she was concerned about her husband's diet.

"Are you suggesting that my father and your mother were in love and having an affair?" he asked, stunned.

"No, I am not insinuating anything, nor am I implying such a thought. What I am saying is that our parents were having something, and they were happy with that something."

I remember my dad going to Goldsmith's Department Store in Memphis for a few days. He stayed at the Peabody Hotel, the best in town . . . That was not like my dad. Pop never went on the road to see a customer. He would never go to the best hotel and spend that kind of money. I also remember two days in Baltimore and three in Miami. His mind raced. He smiled. "It looks like our parents were a hot couple."

"It's only the beginning. I'm glad you are sitting down."

Eric called, "Waitress, can I have a Dewar's on the rocks?"

"Make it two," Anthony added. They clicked glasses and Anthony continued.

"My mom was so taken with Haskell, and the thought of his suggestion to print a menu and give it to customers for call-in orders. Earlier, I told you it was my idea. I was not planning to tell you this story. Mom thought he was a genius. Her business doubled, no—tripled. And then he suggested she order boxes to put the pizzas into, and your father recommended your printer to do the job. And there are two more steps your genius dad produced. Mom hired two boys for the evening to deliver the pizzas. And are you ready? Do you know we have five Gina's Pizza shops, here in the city and Brooklyn? The first one was your father's idea, with—now get this—he lent Mom five thousand dollars. And she paid him back."

"Holy shit. My father was moonlighting and running our company at the same time."

Anthony nodded. "Yes."

"Is there more?"

Anthony nodded again. "One day her cousin, my second cousin, Salvatore Tracci, head of the Staten Island mob, came into the original Gina's restaurant, where you and your dad always ate. My mom was quietly happy to see him. She did not approve of his line of business, but he was family, which is an especially important commitment for all Italians who migrated from the old country."

"Was he hungry? What did he want?" Eric was curious. *And what could this have to do with my father?*

"Finish your Scotch, you may need another."

"Holy shit." Eric knocked back the drink and ordered a second.

"Our cousin Sal came to the restaurant for advice. He knew Momma was now running a successful business. In fact, he knew it was a booming, lucrative restaurant company. And it was legitimate. He came to her for advice. He wanted her to guide him into a straight and honest deal. His children were getting older. He didn't want the same life for them. He wanted college and all the rest."

Eric sat mesmerized. "What advice did she give him?" he whispered.

"She didn't give him any advice. She said she would get back to him."

"Don't tell me. Please do not tell me that she went to my father?"

Anthony nodded. "Your father was fascinated by the idea of giving advice to the mob."

"Take another sip of your Scotch," Anthony urged his friend. They clicked glasses.

Both men sat quietly. Neither spoke for thirty seconds, all heavy with questions.

"Don't sit there with a smile on your face," Eric finally said. "Let's hear it. It sounds like a novel."

Anthony flipped a pack of Newports from his pocket. A single cigarette popped through the opening. He clicked a lighter and lit it.

Through his slightly glassy eyes, Eric put the whiskey glass to his lips and sipped. Both men were just an inch off balance. They were not drunk, just a bit wobbly, with silly grins. One with the story he was going to recite, the other with an expectation of a secret father.

Still, before he heard a single sentence, Eric felt a mix of excitement and disbelief. Images he had long forgotten resurfaced.

CHAPTER 57

TEN YEARS EARLIER

Sal Tracci, a big boss in Staten Island, arrived at the Abraham & Haskell suit factory. He wanted to meet his cousin Gina's friend and buy a few suits. The former was a plan to connect with this interesting businessperson, and the latter was a gesture of linking up and trust.

Sal bought four suits and a topcoat. The total came to $230, which he withdrew from his breast pocket and paid with two fifties, five twenties and three tens. As he opened his jacket for the cash, Haskell's heart jumped. He saw a holster and a revolver.

Sal saw the change in the man's face, and a tick of slight fear in the twitch of his eyebrow. "Not to worry," he said. "It's only for protection. I've never used it."

"It frightens me. I've never seen a gun or touched one."

Sal removed the gun from his pocket. "Here, Mr. Brodsky, touch it, hold it. It won't bite you."

His heart beating hard, a slight tremble in his hand, Haskell touched the instrument with his fingertips.

"No, no, grab it." And for the first time in his life, Haskell put a revolver in his hand. He was unimpressed. It was like a toy, but a dangerous toy to play with.

"Is it loaded?"

"No, and never has been."

"So how does it protect you?"

"The sight of it protects me. You saw the gun; I saw the tremble in your hands and the twitch in your eyebrow. Am I safe?"

Haskell nodded his affirmation.

"Haskell, I want us to be friends. My cousin Gina admires and respects you. In fact, she likes you a lot."

"Come into my office," Haskell said, and gestured to his office door. They sat in the other room, out of earshot of everyone.

"Mr. Brodsky, I hear that you are a very smart businessman. I am here for advice. In fact, I would be grateful if you would be my 'business consigliore.'"

"Mr. Tracci, I am not a, what did you call it, a consigliore. I am a men's clothing manufacturer. It's as simple as that."

"Not accurate," Tracci said. "It was you who gave my cousin all the advice on how to grow and expand her pizza business. You knew all the important ideas that link cash, growth, and investment. I need your help. I want to legitimize my life for my children's sake. Please help me. You will never regret it."

Haskell sat back, settling in his chair, taking a deep breath. He had heard those words many times. And he knew all those who believed them always ended up regretting it. He sat in silence looking into Sal's face with apprehension and exhilaration. This was the Mafia asking him for help.

"OK, tell me, what's on your mind?"

Sal put a pack of Chesterfields on the table.

"Sorry, Mr. Tracci, no smoking here."

"You're the boss. Here's my story. You know my business. I always did well, as did my group. But now my kids are getting older. My son has agreed to go to college. It wasn't easy, but he agreed. My daughter is maturing, and soon she will be a woman. I don't want my kids to be ashamed of their father. I want to go into a legitimate, straight business. And as much as I hate it, I will even pay taxes."

Haskell smiled at Sal's honesty. "I will consider helping you, but only if we make rules that you give your word you will never break."

Sal nodded. "I agree; you have my word."

Haskell did not smile or show any sign of fear. "The rules are, you can never come here, no telephone calls, no letters, and no notes. Nothing—anything else is a deal-breaker."

"Agreed," Sal responded steadily, without hesitation.

"Tomorrow we'll meet at Hammer's restaurant on Union Square. It's a kosher restaurant. For sure, no one will know you."

Sal shook his head. "Very sharp, very sharp. The rumors are right. Jews are smart."

CHAPTER 58

THE DEAL

Anthony continued telling Eric his story. "At first, your father was not sure collaborating with the mob was smart. He knew he would never get involved. And as Sal Tracci told my mother, your dad was brilliant. He thanked her many times for the introduction to your father.

"Haskell felt a little excited working with Tracci. Your father told Sal, 'No guns in your pocket, no huge amounts of cash in my pocket.' Both were too dangerous, and Sal agreed.

"The next step Haskell advised was for Tracci to take all the cash he had and put it into a briefcase, like a regular businessman. He then advised Tracci to go to Italy, Germany, the UK. His idea was to make deals with all the great car companies and open dealerships in New York, Connecticut, and New Jersey. The venture was successful. And from out of nowhere, all the mob bosses wanted in.

"Tracci refused, as he had promised your father. He did introduce your father to the bosses. What is difficult to believe is that Haskell was excited. He found the meeting with these guys an adventure. For sure, he never got involved. Just gave advice.

"Now, get this. Your father advised the three biggest bosses to go into the trucking business and the garbage business, and to build casinos in Las Vegas. And most important, he advised them not to cheat their customers or business partners, and to pay their taxes.

"He reminded them that Gambino did many bad things: Murder Incorporated, dishonest ventures, prostitution, all of which he never got in trouble for. Except one venture: he didn't pay his taxes. That was his end. They all listened and took his advice."

Eric held up his hand. "That's enough. I don't want to know any more. I can't believe that my father was having an affair with your mother, working with the mob, and running our business and our family at the same time."

Anthony took another drink from his whiskey glass, smiled, and said, "Are you ready for the best, the most incredible of all things?"

Eric looked down, about to say, "No." Silence followed.

"OK, OK, tell me."

Anthony reached out and took a piece of bread from the table and continued. "Haskell earned the title of Il Padrino Degli Affari Intelligente, The Godfather of Smart Business."

Anthony stopped. That was the entire story. His last revelation was not a surprise. Anthony looked around the room to see if anyone was listening. Leaning across the table, he whispered, "When that moron Marco put the hit on your father, the entire organization went crazy. Meyer called Alberto, instructed everyone to get rid of Marco. A big reward was on the table. And it was done."

They both rose from the table; Anthony took the check. In silence, they embraced, and then they left.

CHAPTER 59

AND LAST BUT NOT LEAST

Melissa, Ben's new secretary, called into his office, "Mr. Brodsky, there is a young gentleman here who wants to see you." Ben sat for a moment then asked, "Does he have a name?"

Melissa turned to the visitor. "What is your name, sir?"

"Harris Brodsky," he replied.

"His name is Harris Brodsky," she told Ben.

He smiled, shaking his head. "Send him in."

Young Harris entered Ben's office. The elder man's hand moved out to greet and welcome the young man.

"Please have a seat. My inner voice told me that someone like you would show up sometime soon," Ben said. "Tell me who you are exactly and what's on your mind."

A moment of silence followed.

"I am Harris Brodsky, your uncle."

Both men smiled. Ben stood up, a grin on his face. "Glad to meet you, Uncle Harris."

The young man began, "Your grandfather Haskell was my father. My mother's name is Gina. She was the Pizza Queen."

Ben rose, stepped around his desk, and embraced what he hoped was a new member of the Brodsky family. Still, he was cautious.

Harris moved back a step. "I want to prove that I am who I say I am. I welcome blood tests, and I will answer any questions you may want to ask me to prove I am who I say I am."

Ben was impressed with Harris's up-front approach, and his mind raced. *To begin with, he looks exactly like his father. His voice and movements are exactly the same.*

"If everything you say is true, what are looking for? Do want us to be friends, cousins? Join us at our Shabbat dinner? Tell me."

Harris reached out and touched Ben's wrist. "I want everything you said. I want be part of the family I lost when murderers took my father's life. I want to join the family business. I want no special favors. I will work hard and do what I am called on to do. The only special favor I hope for is working with you. To learn from you all that you learned from your life in Asia and your early days at Abraham & Haskell."

Harris's prepared speech blew Ben away. And so, all the tests were taken and Harris's history at school reviewed. Haskell had also left a huge investment in a family account to Gina. The blood test gave proof that Harris was a Brodsky.

And lo and behold, my father, Haskell, left a heritage of young men and women who sustained the intellect, work ethic, and ongoing success of poor immigrants who, in their hopes to escape their life of pogroms, hatred, and fear, created a life for themselves and the generations that followed.

TO MY READERS

It was a pleasure authoring this story.
I hope you enjoyed the read.

—Seymour Ubell, author

www.ingramcontent.com/pod-product-compliance
Lightning Source LLC
Chambersburg PA
CBHW050310110726
47899CB00007B/2181